Name, Place, Animal, Thing

Name, Place, Animal, Thing

DARIBHA LYNDEM

ZUBAAN
128 B Shahpur Jat, 1st Floor
New Delhi 110 049
Email: contact@zubaanbooks.com
Website: www.zubaanbooks.com

First published by Zubaan Publishers Pvt. Ltd 2020

10 9 8 7 6 5 4 3 2

ISBN: 978 81 94760 50 4 (hardback)
ISBN: 978 81 94760 51 1 (ebook)

Zubaan is an independent feminist publishing house based in New Delhi with a strong academic and general list. It was set up as an imprint of India's first feminist publishing house, Kali for Women, and carries forward Kali's tradition of publishing world-quality books to high editorial and production standards. *Zubaan* means tongue, voice, language, speech in Hindustani. Zubaan publishes in the areas of the humanities, social sciences, as well as in fiction, general non-fiction, and books for children and young adults under its Young Zubaan imprint.

Typeset in Baskerville 11/13 by Jojy Philip
Printed and bound at Thomson Press India Ltd.

For my father-in-law,
P.K. Singh

Contents

Bahadur

We lived in a house at the bottom of a hill. We took it on rent from Mrs Guha, the lady who lived in the much larger house at the top of the hill. Hers was a lovely Assam-type house that was in several stages of dilapidation, but not so ramshackle that it could not be called quaint. Every time I would go with my father to pay the monthly rent, I would try to peek inside Mrs Guha's house from the front door. 'Stay out here,' my father would warn me as I walked in with him, hoping to get a glimpse of her living room. From the outside, as I stood on my toes, craning my neck, I could see wooden ceilings and floors, as well as a large glass cabinet that housed bric-a-brac which had managed to escape the film of dust that rested gravely on all the books that lay on top of the cabinet. Inside were souvenirs from faraway places and old framed photos of a bygone time. I imagined her travelling to Morocco or Chile, haggling with a street vendor, buying these things; artefacts that were a testimony to a well-travelled life. Proof of travel is as important, if not more important than the actual journey.

My mother, father, younger sister and I lived in that small rented house till I was eight. It was located in Nongrim Hills, a quiet neighbourhood which was at the time considered well-removed from the city centre. The doors were so low that my giant of a father would have to stoop every time he got in. He would only be able to stand straight once he was inside. There was a living room, two bedrooms, a kitchen that only one person could stand in at a time, and one bathroom. The living room was a soothing yellow which was juxtaposed against the riot of colour my mother had adorned the walls with. There were wall hangings made of red fabric, studded with small glass mirrors, that my mother got in Gujarat. Near the entrance, she hung decorative cloth parrots on a string. We had small pieces of furniture placed strategically so no one would bump into them. In a small corner of the room, there stood a large peacock wicker chair, on which she had placed a colourful woollen crochet blanket. We always took our family photographs around it. Nothing in the room matched anything else, which is how my mother liked it. My sister and I never thought the house was small because we never knew anything else.

It was when we were living in this house that I met Bahadur and his family. My earliest memory of Bahadur was of him answering Mrs Guha's summons. I saw this the first day when my father went over to sign the lease. I waited in the garden and picked at ants with a stick as they completed the formalities inside. When they were done and my father was sipping the last dregs from the teacup, she walked to the balcony and shouted out:

'Bahadur! Bahadur! Where are you? Come quickly, it's time to go to Iewduh.'

'Yes! Yes! I'm coming,' Bahadur replied from a distance, breathing heavily as he ran up the slope in his worn-out sandals. I saw him knock his heels against each other like a tap dancer once inside the car, loosening the dry mud that stuck to the soles. He then parked outside the house and waited to take Mrs Guha to the market. It was an old grey Ambassador that seemed to lumber on like an aging rhino let out to graze.

'I don't like how you make me wait,' Mrs Guha said as she fussed over her shawl and got into the car. He kept quiet, smiled and nodded. He knew saying anything would only anger the old lady.

Mrs Guha only left the house on Saturdays when she had to go to the Iew to buy supplies, and she only went with Bahadur. There was no one else who would go with her. She lived alone. She used to live with her husband until he took his place among the bric-a-brac in a small Chinese urn that rested quietly in the back of her glass cabinet. She had two daughters; one was married, staying elsewhere, and the other was studying abroad. She only had a cleaning lady and a cook who would come in the mornings.

It struck me as odd that such a little old lady could stay all alone in this big, quiet house. The only noise in the house would come from the creaking of the wooden floors, which seemed to begin their own private conversation anytime they were disturbed, annoyed perhaps at being woken. Mrs Guha always threw parties where other old biddies would come over to play bingo, sitting around the fireplace with brandy. She was a jolly sort when she was in this state, and one could forget that in the mornings, she was a stodgy old lady who did not like it when the rent was not paid on time.

'I don't like to wait for the rent, you know. My husband would manage things when he was alive, but I'm too old to be coming and knocking at your door,' she would tell my father; and he, on cue, would smile and nod. She would continue, 'If my daughters were here I would have had some help. But they need to leave their home because they have to take care of their husbands'.

Again we would nod and look sympathetic. 'You're doing a great job on your own,' my father always replied. It was as if she waited for him to say this every time, like a petulant toddler waiting to be consoled. The refrain managed to gratify her, although she made a show of pretending she was already well-aware of what he was telling her. She would wave her hand as if to brush off the compliment but would stop grumbling at us. My father always winked at me as soon as we left, as if to let me in on the trick. When I grew older, I used it on my own grandmother.

Mrs Guha owned much of the land on the hill and it was all looked after by Bahadur. It was a large wooded area that was interspersed with houses. The Mohantys and the Kharsyntiews lived in houses adjacent to ours. The Lyngwas and the Hazarikas lived opposite us. There were two large gates, one on the east side and one on the west, and a driveway that went all the way down to our house. Small homes lined the side of this road, and although their construction was never really planned, their even placement side by side was quite fortuitous. The area was so large that there were swathes of land that remained barren. Mrs Guha could not afford to build more houses there, but she was loath to sell the land that had been in her family since before Meghalaya had seceded from Assam.

Bahadur worked as the guard, gardener, driver and

caretaker, all rolled into one. The place would be in shambles if not for him. He made life more comfortable for everyone around him. I heard the residents complain and call to him for numerous reasons: 'Bahadur, my pump'; 'Bahadur, there are rats in the house'; 'Bahadur, can you paint my windows?' Everyone went to him. Sometimes when they were happy with his work they would treat him to a beer or give him bakshish, or 'boxes' as my grandmother called it. Each morning as I was on my way to school, I would see Bahadur sweeping leaves and dust with his rake-like bamboo broom in the Mohantys' perpetually overgrown lawn. Through the cloud of dust I would shout, 'Bye Bahadur!' waving my hand frantically so he would see me. In the evenings he washed Mrs Kharsyntiew's car and watered Mrs Lyngwa's plants. I would see him stick one end of a water hose into a little tap that was fixed to a wall near Mrs Kharsyntiew's house, from which spring water trickled through. Sometimes I ran back home from school so I could help him water the plants, although my spindly arms could barely hold the watering can.

Whenever I saw Bahadur, he was always busy. It was only in the evenings that he could spend time with his family, but he never missed a meal with them. He and his family lived in a shanty behind the house we stayed in. It had one big room in which they all slept, ate and entertained guests. Next to this room was a tiny kitchen. Outside their house was a place where they could bathe and wash clothes in the open. Twenty paces away from this spot was an outdoor toilet. It seemed to me that they had been living there for a long time.

I once asked my mother, 'Why is Bahadur's Khasi so strange? He cannot say "doh" Mom, he says "du-oh."'

'He's not Khasi, that is why he cannot pronounce it like we do. It's a third language to him. He's Nepali.'

It was only after my mother said this that I began to notice other dissimilarities between us. Bahadur did not look like us or speak like us, but I never thought he was very different. His rice pudding was as good as the one my mother made, and he liked watching movies just as we did.

Bahadur was slight in stature and looked as though he had spent too much time in the sun. His eyes crinkled when he smiled. Crusty bits of paint stuck to his trousers and a woollen cap always sat snugly on his head, no matter the season. Once, I saw him carry a Sintex tank all by himself, and I was surprised he was so strong for such a small man. I think he was forty then, and he had been working here since he was a child. His father, before him, worked for the late Mr Guha, Mrs Guha's father-in-law.

Bahadur and his wife had five children: four daughters and one son. At the time I started to become friends with them the eldest, Suman, was sixteen, then there was Rupa who was thirteen; Jyoti was eleven, Ashwini was nine and Ajay was seven, the same age I was then. They were my closest friends in the early days of my childhood, before I met Yuva, who would later become my closest friend. Bahadur made it a point to send all of his kids to school. Every morning before the sun rose, he went out to the colony where the milkmen stayed, to buy milk for his family. His wife woke him up and handed him two canisters and a fine piece of muslin to strain the milk. He always bought more than was needed so his children could drink their fill before they went off to school. 'Don't spoil them so much,' his wife would tell him every so often, but I think she was secretly happy that he went out of his way to care for them.

My father and Bahadur got along very well. He called my father 'Bajrang' because he had heard some of the neighbours calling him 'Bah Jrong'. 'Bah Jrong' was a nickname our neighbours gave my father which loosely translates to 'Mr Tall'. My father, a Catholic, found Bahadur's name for him humorously ironic, so he never bothered to correct him. Bahadur would sometimes accompany my father whenever he had business outside town. He would take the wheel when my father got weary. Bahadur enjoyed the excursions, and my father was glad for the rest his company accorded him on the long drive home.

One time, I was allowed to go along with them. On the journey back I heard Bahadur telling my father about his problems:

'Madam does not pay me very well, but at least I get that shanty free of rent,' he said to my father.

'You could try asking her for more money,' my father suggested.

'No, no she will get angry. Right now my family has a roof over their heads and that is important. Why should I anger the old lady. She said she would look after my family. She promised me. Especially for Suman.'

'How? How will she help her?'

'Her daughter in foreign, she needs someone who will take care of the baby.'

'What baby? Her daughter just got married and is still studying.'

'Oh when she has it. She told me this. Suman is getting older, and I don't know if I can afford a wedding. Madam promised she would take care of her.'

'Hmm, don't put too much hope in this plan,' my father warned him. Bahadur nodded and took over the wheel.

Every evening after I had finished my lessons, I would go outside Bahadur's house and call out to my friends to come and play. At sunset the earth still smelled of fresh wet soil as a result of the rains. It always rained. The flying termites would crowd around the porch lights after the rains, looking as if they were drying themselves by the warm yellow glow of the bulb. They came out in swarms after the rains, an exodus, looking to start their colonies elsewhere, many losing their wings, crawling frantically on the ground, away from the curious sniffs of the cat who prowled around. As I waited for my friends at dusk, shouting their names—'Suman! Rupa! Ajay!'—I would swat away the hapless flying termites that would land on my shirt. Those nights were cool, the wind blowing against my skin making all my hair stand on end, reminding me of how a dead chicken's skin would look after Bahadur had plucked all its feathers out in the backyard, before it was to be cooked. The days preceding these nights would get very sultry, and the clouds would look grey and bloated. When they were ready, they burst out, a hard thundering rain, splattering the hills, washing away the dust. It looked like the hills had just been given a fresh coat of green paint. The streets would get muddy, and the asphalt road would be riddled with circular rainbow patterns from the rain mingling with the oil that dripped from cars. Outside our house the unpaved ground oozed with sludge. I would stand there and wait, my rubber slippers sinking into the squelchy mud, the wet grass coming up to my ankles and the flying termites getting in between my eyes and my spectacles. After a while I would see my friends all come out and wave. We would play hide and seek in the grassy wooded area behind our houses until it was too dark to see, and I could hear my mother calling out for me, 'Da! Da! Come back home! It's time for dinner!'

I often went to Bahadur's home on the weekends. Even though I had already had lunch in my own home, I had a second one with them. They nearly always ate the same thing: dal, rice and a single fresh onion that stung each time you bit into its purple, crunchy flesh. We would all sit on the floor in a circle. 'This is like a picnic,' I told them once, to which they just shrugged and smiled. 'Bam, bam,' Bahadur's wife would coax me into eating before the dal got too cold.

I don't remember enjoying any meal as much as I did the ones I had sitting on the floor of that one-room house, where I did not have to worry about spilling on the carpet or talking too loudly. I could just sit and joke with Bahadur's children, as we took turns biting into the fleshy large onion we all shared. He always apologized that he had nothing more to offer. 'Don't mind beta, it is only this. No meat. Hope that is fine.'

'Yes! I love onions! Also, Mom always makes the dal too thick,' I would say.

'This house is not fit for entertaining guests,' he would continue, and I would reassure him that I did not mind. I knew it was smaller than my house, and that gave me a sense that there was a hierarchy in the world.

Sometimes on warm, dry nights, my mother would open the doors of the room we kept our television in and play an old Bollywood film. Both the doors were opened outward, and the television was brought forward to the front door so that everyone could see. My friends and I would sit on the stairs in front of the house, shaded by a giant weeping willow, its leaves drooping down, almost tickling us. Next to it stood the tall symmetrical cryptomeria tree. It was tall and sturdy, its leaves imbued with a fresh woody smell, and I always took a big whiff whenever I crossed it. It was not a tree that was native to to the region; I was told it was brought by the British a long time ago and planted here. So on the stairs, under the weeping willow and the cryptomeria, we sat in the evenings watching old films as the crickets whittled their feet and the trees rustled. We were enthralled as we watched *Khoon Bhari Maang* or *E.T.*, rooting for the heroes, gasping at every turn. Sometimes a caterpillar would fall off the tree onto our necks, causing a breakout of red rashes. Suman always used her long hair to try and rub off the caterpillar's hair that stuck to our skin. 'Here take one end of my hair,' she offered.

'I think I should just ask mom to pull out these things with tweezers,' I said pointing to the little spiky hairs on my skin.

'No this will work. I always do this and it removes all of them,' she insisted. It worked most of the time.

End of school term holidays were for playing and 'gallivanting', as my mother chided when she was in bad spirits. We played in the meadow behind our homes. I was not sure if it was part of the property. There was a barbed wire fence that ran along the periphery of the meadow. It was all warped and bent wide enough for a person to go through. We squeezed ourselves through these openings. In this meadow, men lay on the grass shirtless, sunning themselves as their goats grazed. On bright mornings we could get a clear view of the meadow from the steep slope that lay on one side of the west gate. This gate opened to a part of the property that had fewer houses. We would go there to play because we knew we would not be bothered by adults. The ground was at its driest in the winter, and we took advantage of this. We all carried our pieces of cardboard to this slope and pretended these pieces were toboggans, climbed to the top and came sliding down. Someone always ended up tearing their trousers.

Bahadur left soon after I turned eight. I had heard him tell my father that he missed being back in Nepal, and that he longed to see his mother before she died. His longing for his village was further exacerbated by what happened to his son about a month after my birthday.

I did not know everything that transpired that day. I only caught glimpses of what had happened in the morning by peeking out onto the street through the lace curtains that hung against the window. The rest I learnt by overhearing snippets of conversations between my parents.

Like on any regular day, my mother and father woke up at five in the morning for a steaming cup of tea. On most days, my mother would be very loud when she busied herself in the kitchen, and I would wake up to the sound of the kettle being put on the stove noisily. With nothing but the sound of birds chirping and the milkmen dropping off canisters outside doors, they sipped tea and calmly discussed the things that needed to be done that day. On this morning as they continued their conversation, the quiet was pierced by ghastly cries for help. My parents ignored them at first until the sounds grew louder and louder. The cries sounded like they were coming from a wounded animal. My father came into the room we were sleeping in to peek outside, trying to detect the source of the sound. His presence woke me up, and I sat upright on my bed to also look outside my window. I heard my father exclaim 'My god!'; he rushed out to call my mother and tell her what he had seen. She told him, 'Hurry up! Get dressed and go help him!'

The urgency in their voices scared me and I tried harder to get a look at what they had seen. My father put on his shoes and some warm clothes and ran out. That is when I saw him, it was Ajay, and he seemed to be covered in blood. He could not even stand. I saw my father run toward him, trying to hold him steady. My father shouted to a man that happened to pass by, calling to him for assistance. I could see him gesturing, asking the man to stand with the boy as my father went to look for Bahadur. He was not around, and it was only his wife who was home. Bahadur had gone to get milk. The family ran back to where Ajay was; he seemed in a worse condition than when my father had left him in. On seeing him bloodied and moaning, his mother was beside herself with shock and needed to be consoled. His legs and his hands bore wounds and he bled onto the asphalt road.

On hearing the noise, other neighbours came to their windows to ascertain what had happened but, as I watched, they did nothing to help. Mrs Kharsyntiew, who lived with her three sons, peeked through the window while all this transpired. I saw the ruffle of the lace curtain being pulled back abruptly by someone in that house. They did not bother to come out.

I saw my father go towards Mr Mohanty's house and ring the bell. He shouted, 'Can Mr Mohanty come and help please? I cannot lift the boy alone, and I don't have a car.'

Mrs Mohanty opened the door and replied abruptly, 'He is sleeping.' She shut the door just as abruptly.

The Purkhayastas and the Lyngwas also watched from their windows. I saw my father try to wave at them when he could see movement through the windows, but no one responded to him or came outside. The passerby who had been standing with Ajay and the family then offered his help. He and my father bent down to try to pick Ajay up without causing him any pain. We did not own a car so they had to carry Ajay all the way out to the main road to hail a taxicab. None of the neighbours offered their vehicles. There was a deathly silence on our hill except for Ajay's loud wails.

I did not see my father for a few hours. When he got back, we were all sitting in the kitchen. He came and slumped into a chair. He looked exhausted. My mother made him some tea and after he had taken a few sips, he proceeded to tell my mother what had happened. 'That boy was mauled by dogs. He was throwing stones at them trying to get their attention, but he angered them instead. Must have been around fifteen dogs. They all bit him pretty badly. Bahadur came there as soon as he got word.'

My father took another sip of his tea and shook his head. 'No one came to help that boy. Neither Mohanty's son came to help nor any of Kong Kharsyntiew's three boys. They all just watched from their windows. They could have offered to come with us. What is the world coming to if neighbours won't even show a shred of decency and help out a young boy?'

'What about Ajay?' My mother asked, looking worried.

'He'll need stitches and shots. He was badly bitten. He can barely stand. Bahadur was panic-stricken when he got to the hospital, he did not know what to do. It was a good thing we were there.'

'I can only imagine. At least that other chap was there. Who was he?'

'I don't know who he was,' my father replied, looking perplexed. 'He happened to be taking a walk in the area. Decent fellow. I don't know how I would have managed without his help. Tariang, his name was. Stays in Jaiaw. I was surprised when he told me he was from there.'

'What was he doing so far off from there?'

'Some football training or some such. Didn't ask him too many questions.'

'Surprising to see a Jaiaw boy help out a dkhar,' my mother remarked, almost chuckling as she mentioned a part of Shillong that was only inhabited by Khasis, 'Bloody Mohantys didn't come out to help. They were the closest to him.'

'Most people see Bahadur as the help, and they don't want to lift a finger for them.' My mother looked sombre.

'Dkhar' was a word I learnt when I was young. I did not understand its full meaning until I was much older. It refers to people like Bahadur and Yuva, people who were not like me, who were not tribal. I understood it to mean people who were not from this land. It was a strange, loaded word meaning different things to different people. Words like dkhar can be innocuous or they can be weaponized. It made me think of people in terms of them and us. Although I was not taught it as an insult, I always saw it used as one.

We finished our breakfast and I was told to go to my room. My parents continued with the discussion once I was gone and all I could hear was steady mumbling. I felt terrible for Bahadur and his family. I prayed for Ajay to get better. In our room, my sister sat with her toys oblivious to what had happened, too young to understand. I tried to ask my father some questions that evening, 'How many stitches did Ajay have to get, Papa? Is he going to be fine? Why didn't anyone else help him?' My parents reassured me that Ajay was fine and changed the topic. I knew enough not to ask any of my friends, and I was told to let them have their privacy. I felt alone and confused because I had no one to talk to and I worried about them.

In the weeks that followed this incident I rarely saw my friends. They had to help around the house because

Bahadur and his wife were too busy taking care of Ajay. Mrs Guha, although sympathetic, did nothing to help. The neighbours neither asked Bahadur about Ajay, nor offered any assistance.

With time, Bahadur grew jaded. I never saw him help any of the other neighbours anymore, or sit with any of Mrs Kharsyntiew's boys on warm winter mornings, cleaning their lawn and drinking beer like he used to. He spoke very little and only went out with Mrs Guha when she had to go shopping. Lunches in his home were no longer how they used to be. He looked quiet and pensive, and barely responded to what his children were saying. He would only nod when we all sat down for our meals, smiling at me weakly when I left and waved goodbye.

When Ajay had recovered fully, Bahadur felt like he could no longer work there. He came over one evening to speak to my parents and told them how he was grateful for all their help and that he would soon be leaving. 'I miss my family in Kathmandu. All my brothers are there,' he said to them.

'But what will you do there?' My mother asked.

'My cousin brother owns and runs a garage there. I can learn about cars. He will teach me.'

My parents tried to convince him to stay, but Bahadur was adamant.

Before they left, I met my friends for one last night when we sat to watch a Bollywood film on the steps. We picked *Khiladi*. It was a chilly night and there were no caterpillars then. The stairs felt cold underneath us, and we all had our own shawls. That night Bahadur and his wife joined us as well. My mother made tomato soup with croutons that floated at the top—my favourite. We all sat there drinking soup out of small cups, watching the film and enjoying their last night at Mrs Guha's.

Long after we moved away from Mrs Guha, I heard that she had relocated to Wisconsin in the United States to live with her daughter. She had sold the property and most of her things, except for the photographs that hung on the wall, the items in the glass shelves, and the Chinese urn that housed the remains of her husband. She carried those wherever she went. I never found out who bought the property. I often crossed it on my way to college and from the rusted gated where the green paint was chipping off, I could only see tombstones. I heard that the land had been turned into a graveyard. There were no longer any signs of the house we stayed in, no doorway with its low entrance, no weeping willow or cryptomeria tree from which the caterpillars fell. The ramshackle cottage that housed my earliest friends and shaped my memories lay bare and forgotten. Only the flying termites remained, fluttering below the street lights outside the property. They came out of their hidey holes in the ground after it rained, their thick bodies carried by shiny papery wings, lured by any source of light, hypnotized—until they collapsed and died on the soggy yellow leaves and soft red earth below.

Mr Baruah

I had seen him walking alone at dusk. I had seen him, his head bowed as if weighed down by his thoughts, his eyes transfixed on his feet. He walked slowly, talking to himself, as he avoided bumping into people on the street. He was very pale, tall and lanky; his hair greasy and unkempt, almost covering his face like ivy over walls. I would see him come out only after five in the evening, just when it was beginning to get dark. I had never seen his face in the sunlight. It was hard to tell how old he was, but I would call him 'Uncle' when I would see him go down to his store on my way back home from school. He was not Khasi but a dhkar, so I never called him Bah. He would nod in acknowledgement and smile. 'Baruah,' I had heard people call him.

He ran a little shop that sold cards, stationery, toys and curios. It was a dusty little store at the end of a narrow side street located in Barik, the centre of Shillong. It hardly had any visitors. I suppose he made do because his was the last of the shops in that line to close down. When greeting cards, handwritten letters and postcards started to become an antiquated means by which to keep in touch with your loved ones, many shops such as his slowly began to shut down. Before it shut, though, I would go to his store often. It was a small shop with a weather-beaten pink front door which sealed in the warmth on cold winter days. Cards lined the shelves on two sides of the walls. One wall had shelves that housed every kind of fancy notebook and all the paint supplies one would ever need. We used these books to trace drawings with carbon paper or to play Name, Place, Animal, Thing. There were autograph books with Mickey Mouse and Barbie on the covers, and slam books that were covered in glitter and bows. The walls of the store were an orange hue, which endowed it with a warmth like you were soaking in a warm pot of tea.

Not more than a few people could stand in the store at a time without it getting overcrowded. This happened especially on Valentine's Day. College students would be hovering over the section that sold soft toys and Valentine's Day cards. Some were too embarrassed to ask for what they wanted and could only point to the thing they liked:

'That one, yes, the one with the heart in the centre,' I heard one of the customers say.

Baruah smiled knowingly. 'Ah that's our best one. Would you like it gift wrapped?'

'Yes, sure,' the customer said, nodding and indicating that he was in a hurry, embarrassed to be buying a bear. He waited in a corner, impatiently tapping his feet and fidgeting with his hands. As Baruah was wrapping it, the college student glanced furtively at the customers, hoping he would not be caught by one of his relatives or friends.

Baruah quickly placed the bear in a box and adroitly wrapped it in red wrapping paper, tying a bow with the flourish of an expert craftsman. 'Here you go and hope she likes it,' he said, waving at the teenage boy as he walked hurriedly out the front door, mortified at Mr Baruah for having drawn attention to him. In contrast to this, there were also many boys who bought Valentine gifts in bulk with the ease of seasoned practitioners. Baruah loved it when the store was teeming with people and did his best to help all his customers.

The shop was very close to where I lived and I went there on most weekends, and sometimes after school. I liked going to Baruah's store. I was nine at the time. I was curious about him, and he never had any problem with me spending time there. My mother had no objection to me going; she knew him and his wife well. Every day before she dropped me there she would tell me not to misbehave.

'Don't touch anything. Only ill-behaved children play with things that aren't theirs, and I have taught you better than that,' she said every time she dropped me at the shop.

She never gave me any money when I went, so I could never buy anything. I was only there to look. I had had my eye on a Tweety Bird keychain for a long while, but I was afraid to mention it to her. I would wait for my grandmother to come visit; she was generous and liked to overindulge her grandchildren.

I never went to Baruah's shop on my own. I was of a suspicious nature and would make sure I had the company of my younger cousin if I ever went there. Craig could not even tie his own laces, but if he didn't like someone, he would bite their fingers off. Mr Baruah was nice enough though; he allowed me to flip through the cards on the rack and look at the toys. I helped him while he tended to customers. One time he let me sit at the cash counter; the stool was too high and my legs could not reach the ground but it felt marvellous. Sometimes I got there before him and waited patiently for him to open the store as he fumbled in the cold with the keys and muttered under his breath: 'Which one, which one. Hope I didn't leave it at home.' It was always cold in our town because of the unrelenting rains. I stayed at his store for at least an hour and rifled through the dust-coated baubles that lined the shelves; my mother always picked me up on her way back from the market. I would open all the glossy, shiny cards, the glitter coming off onto my fingers as I read 'Happy Anniversary' or 'Congratulations, it's a Boy!' Some had cartoons in them and I recognized them immediately, deigning to tell my ill-informed cousin Craig which one was Pepe Le Pew and which was Huckleberry Hound. He was seven.

Except for Mr Baruah's store, my mother never really allowed me to go anywhere without her. When I wanted to go rent VCRs from Video Shack, she always accompanied me. Every Friday after school she took me there so I could rent two animated films to watch over the weekend. This was my routine. I had rented *Beauty and the Beast* over ten times. She tried to make me watch other films, and one day she made me rent *The King and I.* I didn't like it as much. The man at the store always knew which ones I wanted. He was a small, bald man with a neat moustache and sunken eyes. He knew where each tape was, even though there were thousands of tapes in his store.

'*Sleeping Beauty* is still out,' he would tell me with the seriousness of a judge passing a death sentence, and each time he said this I was disappointed.

'Can you put it aside for me when you get it back?'

'I could do that but try to come early next time.'

When VCRs and tapes became obsolete, he had to close shop. He runs a travel agency now. He still looks the same. He does not appear to have aged—same bald head, same moustache. I always showed Mr Baruah the tapes when I went into his shop, regaling him with stories of the Little Mermaid and Cinderella.

Mr Baruah kept his store open till nine in the evening, later than the others. In Shillong, shops closed at seven in the evening, so this was very odd. The streets were usually empty by nine. No one ever bothered staying out that late, especially on winter nights when the cold felt like it was hacking all the way through to the bone. I would imagine Baruah walking home alone, the same gait, looking despondent, lost in reverie, his hair covering his face. He shuffled along slowly, till he was swallowed by the fog; the sound of his footsteps fading as the distance between him and his store grew. I imagined his pale face scaring the dogs who came out onto the streets at night to howl at the moon.

On Saturdays, the shutters were down and the store stayed closed. I had nothing to fill the mornings. I grew restless when I had nothing to occupy myself and had to find innovative ways to stay entertained. My cousin Craig was always an accessory to all my plans. He didn't mind listening to my directions and quite liked to be part of the adventures. My mother called it bullying, and I would argue that my cousin was not a simpleton and could not be conned into doing things. 'He knows that he can leave whenever he wants to. I don't force him to do anything. He does everything I ask because he wants to,' I told her when she scolded me for making Craig carry all the stools from the kitchen to the yard one day. My cousin nodded along to everything I said and mouthed 'pardner,' a thing I often called him when I wanted to get into some mischief but was too scared to go in alone.

He liked to take part in all my schemes, but Craig never shared my curiosity about Mr Baruah. Where would he be all day? Was he at home? These questions haunted me whenever I walked past the store and saw the shutters down. He and his wife had moved into town a year ago. They were from Assam, but his wife was a native of Shillong. I knew his house was at the top of the slope next to my aunt's, in Upper Lachumiere. My mother had pointed it out to me one day during a visit to my aunt's. It was a small, nondescript house with a green door that seemed to heave under the weight of the old rickety house. The couple kept to themselves. Their neighbours were curious about them but mostly left them alone. The only grouse they had against the couple was that no one from that house would come out during the monthly jingpynkhuid shnong, when the people of the entire neighbourhood would come out into the streets to clean and tidy up the neighbourhood and surrounding area. This was a practice that everyone living in the community was expected to follow as a good neighbour and Khasi.

But Mr Baruah and his wife remained a mystery for only a short while; soon, people began to discover things about them. In this small town it was easy for people to find out information about one another. It would not be long before gossip would break out. A contagion—rapid, airborne and infectious.

My mother spoke in hushed tones when she first talked about them to her sisters. 'Yes yes, they're both nice people. They ran off together ne?'

'In this day and age it's so silly to stop people from marrying who they want,' one of my aunts said. They all nodded in agreement.

I would sit and listen to them gossip, pretending I was busy reading my novel. All I could gather was that Mr Baruah's mother did not like that he had married a Khasi, Christian tribal. His mother was a devout Hindu.

They had no family here as far as I could tell and lived all alone, just the two of them, I was told. But I only ever saw Mr Baruah leave the house. No one else seemed to go inside. Most times, the curtains of his house remained drawn and there was never any light shining through the windows whenever I crossed his house. Once, I thought I saw the curtains being drawn to the side, a slit small enough for someone to peek through. I felt I saw the flicker of a light and movement. It had sent a shiver down my spine.

One time, I threw a shuttlecock inside their garden on purpose. This was during a bandh when kids could play in the streets. I had decided to play outside their house, hoping I could catch a quick glimpse of who might be inside. When I could not see anyone come out, I took matters into my own hand. As the shuttlecock came towards me, I hit it hard, aiming it sideways so it would go over the wall and into their garden.

'Oh lah dep! I'm not going in there,' my friend Yuva said out loud when she saw where it had gone. Even Yuva thought Mr Baruah strange, as did most of the kids in the colony.

'I'll go and get it,' I replied feigning trepidation. I pulled at the rusty gate, and it groaned at being tugged. I looked at my hands, and there were paint chips and an orange stain across my palm as if the gate was rarely used. I put my nose to it and it smelled like blood, metallic.

Inside, the garden was overgrown with weeds and near

the front door, a lawn chair rested on its side. The house looked uninhabited. I walked to the door and rang the bell. I rang it twice. No one answered. But I knew someone was inside because I had seen Mr Baruah walk in an hour ago. I turned away and started to walk back outside, and then I heard it: an unearthly wail coming from inside. It startled me, and I ran out the gate as fast as I could. On seeing me run out, Yuva followed suit and we sprinted together back to my aunt's, not stopping for anyone or anything.

When we finally stopped, Yuva asked me, wheezing as she talked and clutching her sides: 'What did you see?'

'I didn't see anything. I heard something!' I exclaimed, panting as I said it, my throat hurting.

'What? What did you hear?'

'A wail. Like a banshee!'

'What? Oh god, that's scary. What do you think it was?'

'I don't know but it sounded like it was in pain.'

'See I told you not to go in!' She shouted at me as she slapped me on my arm.

'Ow! All right, I didn't know,' I said, rubbing my shoulder.

We spoke no more about it. We ran inside to my aunt's living room and had the tea and biscuits my aunt had laid out for us.

I knew something strange was going on in that house; the wail I heard confirmed it. Unlike Yuva I could not let it go. I thought about Mr Baruah's house for days after we lost our shuttlecock. I felt I needed answers. So one morning while my mother dropped me to school, I asked her, trying to sound casual, 'Isn't it funny how Mr Baruah only comes to his store in the evenings?'

'I don't know, maybe he doesn't like the sun,' my mother said jokingly.

I drew my breath in sharply. 'I knew it,' I thought to myself. 'She has confirmed my suspicions. I don't even know how she can laugh about this.'

That same morning, I made up my mind, I would go to Mr Baruah after school and confront him. It was up to me. For the sake of my family and my town, I thought. I alone knew the secret that Mr Baruah was so deviously hiding. He was fooling people with his kind words and unthreatening demeanour. I was the only one who could stop him, I thought to myself, hardening my resolve and building courage.

I was almost glad that a person like Mr Baruah chose to come to this town. Nothing exciting ever happened here. 'How would I be a hero and save the town if there was nothing to save it from?' I remember telling Craig one time. Except for the odd tussle between a non-tribal and the Khasis, in my young mind, I felt hardly anything interesting went on in our town.

Later, perhaps two years after I confronted Mr Baruah, Mr Roy would come to our house bleeding from his head. I considered this exciting enough and went to school the next day, feeling important because I had something to tell my friends. This happened when I was much older and living in our house in Rynjah, a home we moved into in the early 90s. Mr Roy was our tenant. One evening on his way back from work, he was beaten up by some boys just outside our house. 'Racially motivated hate crime,' I heard my father tell my mother in the other room. I did not fully understand what that meant then. I had to sit with Mr Roy as my father called the police. The brutalized man was worried about his face and kept asking me for a handheld mirror.

'Beta, how is my face? Is it bad?' he asked me with a pained expression on his face, as he sat with his head tilted up so as to not let any blood drip onto our living room floor.

'It's fine, uncle,' I replied, 'here, take this tissue and wipe the blood off.' I handed him a soft tissue I had brought from my room.

He sopped up the blood on his face near his left eye with the tissue. He did not remove all of it because he still wanted to appear pitiable. Every time he touched the wound, he winced. He was not very badly hurt, only shaken by the ordeal. I found it very amusing to watch him as he groaned and moaned and shifted in his seat as if he had wounds on every inch of his body.

'Can you show me a mirror?' he asked, not satisfied by my report that his face was still intact.

'You're fine uncle,' I said, trying to sound reassuring.

'No no beta, I just want to see.' I obliged him, trying not to giggle. I went up to my room and got an old hand-held mirror that was lying around. I placed it in his trembling hands and watched him as he held the oval mirror to his face and scrutinized the damage.

When this happened, I was excited at first, but looking at the troubled expressions on my parents' faces, I quickly adopted a sombre mood. The people of the neighbourhood along with the local headman decided to put street lights in that lane to avoid such a thing from happening again. Mr Roy soon went back to Calcutta. That was that. Apart from these everyday occurrences of people being mauled by humans or animals, nothing otherworldly ever happened in our lives. That's why perhaps people in this town were so mundane, I thought. No one would believe me if I were to tell them what I had discovered. They would tell me I was only a child. All they were worried about was the rain washing away houses every year during the monsoon. My grandmother used to tell me the rains would stop only if the rain 'bam ia u briew' and took a man's life. I don't know if that's true, but I noticed the rains did once stop after they had pushed a house into a river, causing me to believe that my grandmother was on to something.

A few days after my mother had confirmed my suspicions, I decided to put my plan into action. I wore my best running shoes and carried a Bible in my bag. I made Craig do the same, and we made our way to the store in the evening. I got there at my usual five o'clock and Mr Baruah greeted me warmly. He was putting a plate out as the electric kettle next to him erupted gleefully, filling the room with steam. He enjoyed making his own tea and, on cold winter evenings, would sometimes offer me a cup. The warm amber liquid always felt nice going down my throat as it touched the insides of my cold empty stomach.

'Come come! There are some biscuits on this plate. Why don't you and your brother have some? A relative of mine got them from Germany.' My cousin ran for them, but I stopped him. I pinched his arm and threw him a look so he would not take one. This guy was good, I thought; he knew kids would not resist sweet things. In school we always got excited when we saw goods with a barcode on them. That made us feel like the thing in question was from abroad and hence much better in quality than what we got here. It was hard to say no to biscuits from Germany, but I knew I had to follow the plan so I said a polite, 'No, thank you' and carried on looking at the cards as I watched him from a corner of the room.

Things proceeded as usual and nothing untoward happened for the next hour. I knew, however, that I would soon have to carry out what I had set out to do. As the clock neared six, I began to reach in for the Bible from my bag. Just as I had got it out, words began to fail me and my legs turned to jelly. All the courage I had pumped myself full of, was beginning to escape out of me like air from a leaky balloon. I could not carry forward my plan. I felt scared and a sinking sensation filled the pit of my stomach. My desire to save our town by outing him battled with my memory of the kindness Mr Baruah had shown me. I inched closer to him but every time I tried to speak I felt a lump in my throat like I had eaten a jawbreaker without sucking on it first.

After two failed attempts, I decided that I had to let Craig have the glory of saving Shillong, even if it would mean that I would win no laurels. I put my Bible into his hands, whispered in his ear and told him to carry out the plan as I instructed.

Craig nodded and made his way to the counter. 'Mr Baruah,' he shouted, startling the store owner.

Surprised, Mr Baruah answered, 'Yes?'

Without any preface or warning, putting on the most determined look he could muster, my cousin then baldly asked: 'Are you a vampire?'

I panicked. The boy had forgotten the plan. He was supposed to place the Bible on his chest as he asked, and ease himself into the question. I had told him all this when I had whispered in his ear. All was foiled. I started to strategize a quick escape looking at all the doors and windows even as I started to sweat profusely. But while my mind was running through the many possible scenarios that would ensue, Mr Baruah began to laugh.

With a smile, he said, 'No, I am not a vampire. Why would you ask that?' and ruffled my cousin's hair.

I edged forward as Craig turned to me for support. Mr Baruah's easy answer had left me uncertain of my suspicions, but I said to him defensively, 'Well you only open your store at night, and I was wondering why. I really like you, uncle, but you act very strange and you're always coming out only after dark. What else could I think?'

'Well that's a fair point,' Baruah said as he turned to me, pushing his long hair out of his eyes. 'The thing is, my wife and I have a little baby. She works during the day and someone needs to be there with the baby during the day,' he continued. 'So I'm with the baby all day, and I can only open my store in the evenings.'

Something about his answer rang true, and the banshee wail I had heard at his house suddenly became an ordinary infant's cry. My anxiety began to dissipate.

'Oh, like that,' I replied. I decided that, rather than being disappointed at finding him mundane, I was relieved that he was ordinary, that his inability to leave his home when the sun shone was because of a little baby. He was a caring father, not the undead. I felt silly for having doubted him. I had not wanted to stop coming to his shop.

I inched closer to the table with the biscuits on them while I put my Bible back into my bag. He watched me, amused as he poured himself a cup of tea. No one said anything for a minute till I mustered up the courage to pull the plate towards me.

'Now that that's settled, can I have a biscuit then?' I asked, my voice slicing through the awkward silence.

At which Mr Baruah smiled wide and nodded. Craig and I bolted the rest of the biscuits down while he sat quietly and neatly stacked all the change in his drawer.

The rest of the evening was uneventful and mundane, except for the dog that got into the shop and wreaked havoc with the crayons and pens in the stationery section.

AVVA

The light shone behind the cut-out alphabets, a neon sign which read AVVA. It was the only shop in that lane which could afford to have neon lights. It glowed, a lighthouse, a fuzzy beacon in the dark. On cold foggy nights, from afar, we could see the red haze that emanated from the sign, a soft alphabetical halo. This was a Chinese restaurant, the first of many that would soon spring up in different parts of my town. It was known for its Kolkata-style Chinese meals and most of the town went there before a Dominos or a KFC ever opened up, long before we had even heard of them. AVVA stood in the middle of town, on the side of the highway, between a card shop and a laundry place. The restaurant was always inundated by the footfall of hungry patrons. It was owned by Tommy Lu, a Chinese immigrant who had moved here from Kolkata years ago with his family. 250 years ago his forefathers had moved to Kolkata from China.

It was always a grand occasion when my father decided to take us to AVVA. 'Don't cook today,' my father would tell my mother as if making an announcement in a town square. 'Let's go out to eat.'

'Go get ready. Hurry up! You know how your father and I don't like to wait,' my mother would tell us when this proclamation was made as she pinned up her jaiñsem over her turtleneck sweater. Though the two pieces of cloth were usually worn draped over a blouse, my mother liked to wear her jaiñsems over sweaters because she was sensitive to the cold.

We would hurriedly put on what our mother instructed us to wear and stand by the front door waiting for them. Within half an hour we would be by the side of the road trying to hail a cab as I tugged at my turtleneck sweater whose itchy spines kept prickling my skin. In time, a cab would stop for us and we all would get in, excited to be out late. My father always occupied the front seat as he needed all the leg space he could get. He was six feet three to my mother's five feet nothing.

It was a short drive to AVVA. We would get off on the side of the road opposite the restaurant and cross the road, holding hands, scampering inside. Once inside we would be accosted by sights, sounds and smells. The room was a salmon pink which contrasted with the red cushioned seating at every booth. The walls were lined with framed Chinese watercolours on one side, and on the other side, under the buttery orbs of light, perched a large paper fan like a giant moth. Red Chinese lanterns hung from the top of the ceiling from which the light inside filtered through, their glow causing the room to blush. Moveable screen doors allowed for some semblance of privacy. The shop front windows were darkened by a thick black film that had been pasted on. It did not matter if it was night or day outside, inside it always looked like it was dark out.

My sister and I were always tasked with looking for an empty booth. We would crane our necks as we avoided getting in the way of the waiters who were bringing in their steaming trays to serve the guests. There were five waiters who worked there then. I would smile at all of them when they walked by our table. There were three Chinese waiters, a Nepali and a Bihari waiter. I knew this because Tommy always spoke to them in different languages, sometimes a creolized version of the three. They worked quickly and with an adroitness that ensured the place ran smoothly. No one ever had to wait too long. A towel on one arm and a platter on the other, they dexterously criss-crossed through people coming in and out of the restaurant. They were always in a hurry to place the plates on the tables as if they were scared that their hands would catch fire from the dishes. The two cooks inside were Chinese as well, and they taught the other staff members the tricks of their trade.

I always ordered the chicken noodle soup. I knew what I wanted. 'Order something else em, you can't keep eating the same stuff,' my father said every time he heard what I wanted.

'I like this. I'll try something different next time,' I would reassure my father.

He came to accept that I would only order chicken noodle soup and that that was what made me happy. We ate our fill and there was never enough money left for dessert.

Whenever possible, I would pick the seat facing the door so I could see the other customers as they came in and went. Tommy was always around to greet the people who came to his restaurant. 'Hi, hello, hello,' he would say, repeating himself and grinning as he made small talk.

'You've come? I have not seen you around in a while,' he would say to my father. He said this whenever we visited. Tommy was fond of my father.

'Hello, I've been very busy, but the children are off today so I thought I would bring them here for a little treat,' my father replied.

'Good good, I hope you are doing well?', he asked, turning to my mother, who nodded and replied, 'I'm doing well, thank you'.

Tommy was not above forty years of age. A heavy-set man who wore glasses, he sat behind the counter at the entrance of his restaurant. Whenever he struck up conversation with my father, I would sneak a fistful of the saunf he kept on the counter into my pocket. The chair on which he sat behind the counter was always too low so we could only see him if he was standing up. His face always seemed flushed like he had just come back from a run and I don't remember ever seeing him without his black leather jacket, even in the summer. His wife ran a nail salon, his father was a dentist, and he had two children, a son and a daughter. His father had provided the dentures to my grandmother and his wife would cut my mother's hair whenever she was in the part of the town where the salon was located.

The salon was always full of women. I often waited inside for my mother as she was getting her hair done. I sat in a corner turning page after page of the magazines stacked on the table, women in power suits with large shoulder pads and tightly curled hair stared back at me. A chemical smell permeated the air. A tiny bell at the top of the door always tinkled when someone opened it, and in the time the slow door closer took to get to its original place, the smell of ammonia and shampoo escaped the warm room and tempted the women walking past the shop to take a peek inside. It always smelled that way. Women with small wooden sticks attached to rubber bands on their head sat on revolving chairs, as they flipped through the same magazines. They all looked like innocuous Medusas. I only found out later, when I asked my mother, that those funny sticks were used to perm hair. My mother did not like keeping her hair poker straight because she claimed she liked 'volume'. I hated it when she got her hair permed, so did my father. 'Chee what have you gone and done to yourself,' he said every time he opened the door for her, the wisps at the periphery of my mother's big hair catching the light. He always poked fun at her whenever she came back from the parlour. She remained undeterred and it was not until I was sixteen that she stopped chemically perming it.

The Lu family was a big part of the thriving business community in our very small town. Everyone went to AVVA. The food was comforting and the place was always packed on cold winter days. College students would stand outside the restaurant and take out all the little change they had in their pockets to see if they had enough to share a plate of noodles. Families came in order to get away from home, and couples came so they could be away from prying eyes, sitting in their quiet booths, the light shining through the folding screens colouring their faces a jade green as they shared a bowl of soup.

Tommy was always there to greet them all. He and his family stayed in Mawkhar, which was then mostly populated by Khasis. Chinese migrants in Shillong, unlike some of the other communities, were spread across the city.

Some stayed in Mawkhar, some in Dhanketi and others in Laitumkhrah, Khasi/Jaiñtia neighbourhoods that would have rarely allowed outsiders like Bengalis, Biharis, Nepalis and other migrants. Families like the Lus had integrated well with the Khasi/Jaiñtias in the past, many marrying and starting families with Khasis. I was told that some Chinese families had only left Shillong during the Indo-China War of 1962. My grandmother related to me, 'I went to see the commotion in the square in Mawkhar during that time. They were all being rounded up there so they could be interned and deported. Many Khasis were crying because they did not want to see them go. People tried to discourage me from taking Victor because he was always mistaken for Chinese,' she laughed and said referring to my uncle, her son.

Although welcomed too, Chinese migrants were often still seen as outsiders in Shillong. They worked the typical kind of immigrant jobs: in the food industry, selling apparel and shoes, primping patrons at beauty salons. Some of them like Tommy became successful, while others made enough just to get by. At that time, insurgent groups, such as the 'Saw Dak', saw these thriving, prosperous outsiders as people they could exploit. They were known to collect a 'tax' from outsiders and the Chinese were not exempt.

This became clear when they began to target Tommy and his family. I heard about what had happened by catching snippets of conversations between members of my family.

'They went to his house and asked for money te pha', my grandmother told my aunt.

'Yes I heard kein, ni jing nuid! Any idea how much they asked for?'

'Heard it was a crore but I'm not sure.'

'Will he pay?'

'I don't know. Ni ka pyrthei kam long shuh kum mynshwa,' my grandmother said, lamenting that the world was no longer what it had once been. My aunt nodded and they both sighed heavily as they shook their heads in disbelief.

Another time, I listened as my father and Tommy talked outside a store in Police Bazaar. We had bumped into him, and when my father asked him how he was, Tommy almost burst into tears. 'We have to sell everything and leave. We cannot afford to pay.'

I watched my father listen to Tommy and try to comfort him. I was young at that time and, although I did not know enough about the people who were exploiting Tommy, I knew that he was a nice, honest man. At home, I tried to listen in on conversations about him and what was going to happen to his family as much as I could until the grownups noticed and sent me to another room. They did not like me listening in on their conversations. Sometimes when they turned me out, I pretended to leave and stood by the door, trying to hear what they were saying. They would speak then of the Saw Dak, the powerful group in Shillong who claimed to be fighting for the freedom of the state, for the good of the tribal people. They hoped to secede from India.

'Khynnah dakaid bam don kam don jam,' my grandmother would hiss.

'Ia ki Khasi! As if! They all want to make money,' my aunt added as they spoke of how these men were only looking out for their own selfish interests.

By the time I was old enough to understand their politics, the Saw Dak group became defunct. Bi, my grandmother's helper, was patient enough in those early days to explain to me that the group claimed that they were fighting for the good of the Khasi people. But in the name of doing good, they kidnapped people, shot them point-blank, set their property on fire. They went to the houses of those they considered 'outsiders' and demanded money.

On one occasion, they shot Mr Arora, the car parts shop owner, who lived down the road from my grandmother. One evening as he was locking up at the end of the day, he was shot at close range just outside his shop. He died instantly. He left behind a wife and a young son. I overheard my family discussing that he had been killed because he had failed to pay the weekly 'fees' Saw Dak demanded of him. But a week later it was found that he had in fact paid them, and there had been a mix-up. The group had shot a man who had paid for his safety. I always wondered if they felt any remorse.

Mr Arora's shooting was not a one-off incident. From what I was told and what I remember, shootings were very common in the late 80s and early 90s. Everyone was scared and no one dared to speak up. Those who could afford to pay, did so. Many packed up and left. On days like Independence Day and Republic Day, there would be curfews and bandhs. Cars were set on fire when the group was unhappy with a policy decision the government took. If a minister visited from New Delhi there would be a bandh to protest his coming. In my young mind, I only understood the Saw Dak by the graffiti I saw scrawled across the walls in the city: 'Khasi by blood, Indian by accident'. The group made as little sense to me as the strange writing on the wall.

In school, my friends and I were thrilled at getting a day off school whenever a bandh was announced. We prayed for them whenever we had a test coming up. But for the adults news of a bandh always resulted in panic. On these days I remember my mother scrambling to get to the market to buy food supplies. 'We don't have milk and bread,' she kept telling my father over the phone.

'Mom it's just for one day,' my sister and I reassured her, but she remained stressed.

Across Shillong, families stockpiled provisions even if the bandh had been announced only for one day. I remember though that once a bandh had lasted for four days. We could not go outside on those days. Cars were not allowed to ply the streets, and those that came out in spite of orders had stones pelted at them. Although we were happy about this because it meant we could go out on our bicycles, we soon got bored and missed our friends.

There was also a time when we had to switch off all the lights in the evening on the day of a curfew. I did not know why. I was ten. My younger cousin Craig had just got a new-fangled colouring pencil on which you could change one coloured tip for another. His father had bought it for him on a trip to Mr Baruah's shop. I never got one because it was too expensive. It was pretty and the plastic shined in the light. There were thirty other coloured tips to choose from, and you could see all of them through its clear plastic body. You could take out one tip from its side and replace the tip in use with another one after placing it in the gap created by the new chosen tip. It was brilliant and pretty, and I had not seen anything like it. I so badly wanted to use it, but Craig refused to let me borrow it.

'You don't even draw,' I told him, trying not to sound petulant.

But he was stubborn and did not want to share. The whole evening of the curfew I tried to convince him to lend it to me as we sat around the chawla. Next to me, Bi and the other workers were grinding kwai and tympew on a wooden mortar and pestle for my grandmother. They mixed in shun, and this lime made the paste turn red. My grandmother could not chew the kwai on her own so they had to grind it for her. She kept the paste in a shiny metal box and sometimes I would eat a little bit. The shun made me feel dizzy and warm, and after I had swallowed up all the kwai, I drank water to loosen up the bits of leaf and nut lodged between my teeth.

In the end I fooled Craig into giving the pencil to me. I told him we needed to draw and colour a poster asking the Saw Dak not to throw stones at the house. That we could only use his fancy colouring pencil. That it was imperative.

'It's for our safety. We have to draw this and paste it outside the door. You will be a hero,' I said, knowing this would work on him.

'But why? Why my colouring pencil?' He asked suspiciously as he held the pencil closer to him.

'Because it's the only one that will work. You can even help me draw and paste it. You're young but you can do this. I trust you,' I lied to him and I saw his expression change from one of obstinacy to one of curiosity. After much cajoling, he finally believed me. He gave me his fancy colouring refill pencil and I happily drew a stone with a 'DO NOT THROW' on a piece of paper. I used all the colours in that pencil to paint that stone. He never questioned why the stone was seafoam green. We quickly went to the balcony and we pasted it on the door. We were scared but thrilled, too.

As the years passed, it did get better in Shillong. Mawlai, a neighbourhood which we joked was the den of dkhar-haters, would soften up when dealing with dkhars. But the prejudice was also based on class. The more well-to-do the dkhar was, the safer he was. The worker immigrant had a much harder time. The narrative many Khasis liked to draw was the one of the immigrant Bangladeshis or Nepalis taking their jobs. 'They don't want to do those jobs!' My grandmother said, exasperated when I repeated what I had heard in school about the migrant 'infiltration'. 'Peit how the Khasi contractor works and the dkhar. Half these Khasi workers are always on a chai break or bidi break. Why should I pay them more when they work less?'

There were small clashes that still took place now and then. One time I saw two boys harass a Bengali man driving a Tata Nano. They were accusing him of almost killing them. This was of course an exaggeration because I had seen it happen. He had hit their scooter ever so slightly from the side. No one was hurt. They did make quite a scene, though: 'Nikalo', they shouted at the driver in broken Hindi, 'Abhi nikalo'. The driver was terrified. Luckily some people came over and sorted the matter before it got heated. 'Piet bha next time,' they warned the driver, who nodded vigorously and apologized repeatedly, 'Map Bah'.

Not all dkhars were painted with the same brush. When Amit Paul, the Indian Idol contestant from Shillong, arrived at Police Bazaar for his grand homecoming after being crowned the second runner-up, large crowds gathered to receive him—including those brash boys from Mawlai who enjoyed scaring a dkhar that happened to cross their path. They probably saw him as representing the state in a nationwide competition, and for that he was given a free pass. He had garnered such a following among them that I had heard some even gave him gold as a gift. I still doubted whether Amit Paul would take a stroll down Mawlai.

When it came to him and his family, Tommy wasted no time. He could not predict the behaviour of those men and decided to act quickly. He sold his businesses, packed up his things and went to Kolkata with his family. He sold the restaurant to a Jaiñtia man who would perhaps never have to worry about being hounded or extorted. The police could do little to help because they feared the Saw Dak too. And so Tommy was left on his own.

Before he left, we went one last time to his restaurant. It did not feel the same. Everyone was there to see him off rather than eat a meal. My father went to him and shook his hand. 'Good luck, Tommy. Maybe you can come back when this has died down,' he said trying to sound hopeful.

'I would love that,' Tommy replied, his voice quiet. I felt like I was intruding as I stood there holding my father's hand while he patted Mr Lu on the back.

One by one, everyone shook Tommy's hand before they left. In earlier times it would be him who would go out of his way to speak to his patrons, but this time all of us stopped by the counter to speak to him.

Before he left, Tommy wrote a heart-wrenching open letter that was published in the local papers. He spoke of his love for the town and its people. How he never felt like an outsider and what a pleasure it had been to serve its people. He prayed that he had not offended anyone and said that he would miss this town terribly. People still talk about him. Just like when Chinese families leaving during the 1962 war caused many a heartbreak and sadness, Tommy's family leaving now was a blow to many in the town. He had been a part of our town, known to people, woven into the fabric of our society.

With him gone, AVVA fell into a state of disrepair. The food continued to be good as some of the chefs were retained, but the new owner got rid of the moveable screens and the giant wall fan. The new owner was barely around and the guests were rarely greeted. The neon sign outside stayed the same for a couple of years, and over time the light from one of the shining alphabets fizzled out. They then changed the name, but we still continued to call it AVVA. The new name sounded harsh and reminded us of a dark time. We never did it consciously, it just came easier to us. Sounding out those two syllables—'AV-VA'—harkened us back to a simpler time when I would always order chicken noodle soup and was too short to easily grab a fistful of saunf from the billing counter.

Years later, the restaurant was sold to some other person. He completely renovated the whole place, removing all the old furniture till there was no trace of Tommy and the Lu family ever having owned it, except for the forgotten dusty Chinese lanterns that hung on the ceilings—silent spectators to all that had taken place.

The Yellow Bear

When I was five, my father brought home a yellow bear. The bear was a plush toy that was as big as I was. It was pale yellow with dark eyes, a pink nose and paws padded with rainbow-coloured cloth. It was an expensive Christmas gift. My father was never indulgent, and I always wondered if he gave me this present so as to prove to himself that he could be. He was always reticent with us, so I could never tell.

The bear was the first gift I remember receiving from my father. He took care of me whenever my mother was out of town for work. There was a time when my mother was gone for a month, and in that time I had forgotten all about her. We went to pick her up at the airport when she finally returned. My parents later told me about how I was frightened on seeing her and ran away from the conveyor belt, clutching the toy bear, as she came towards me saying, 'Come here, khun'. They thought it was hilarious. I have no recollection of it. They still tease me about it.

We moved out of Mrs Guha's house in Nongrim Hills when I turned eight. We did not have to pay rent in this new house. It was our own and my bear followed me here. When my father first took us to see it being built, my mother complained that it was in the middle of nowhere. This area, Rynjah, was far away from the city centre. The area was still wooded, with thickets in the surrounding areas that had not been cleared. It would get very dark at night as there were no street lights, and the only lights were the ones that shone through people's windows. You could see shapes moving through the translucent curtains, the only signs of life apart from the dogs that prowled the area. But as the years passed, and Shillong began to grow more populated, houses mushroomed around us. The field in front of our house was levelled and instead of green grass, we saw only the red soil that we tracked into the house sometimes if we ever went to the field. The roads improved as more houses appeared. Later, Rynjah would be considered a posh area in the east side of Shillong after all these improvements had been made.

Ours was a beautiful two-storey house. We lived on the top floor, while the ground floor was let out to tenants. Mr Roy stayed here for a while, until that incident outside our house caused him to move back to Kolkata. The building had no cold stone floors, unlike our first home. The floors and the ceilings were wooden. The house always smelled like polish and wood, and years later, when I left my family home, the smell of Mansion House Polish anywhere would evoke warm memories of my time there. In small nooks of the house my mother lit agarbattis, sticking their thin ends in cracks between the wood. The odorous smoke of sandalwood and rose would waft through these corners, suppressing the smell of the polish. My sister and I groaned when we came home to this smell. 'Smells so dkhar,' we grumbled. 'Only dkhars light so much agarbatti. The house smells bad!'

'So what! I like it,' my mother said defiantly.

My father had designed the house himself and every detail was something he had planned meticulously. He had stacks of interior design books in his cupboard. I sat and went through these on Sunday afternoons when I was bored: volumes of hardbound books, glossy pages filled with pictures and designs. In this house I had my own room. Bear always sat at the centre of my bed, resting his head against the pillows. When I grew older I would use him to cover up all the romance novels which I kept on my bed. My sister's room was next to mine, and she had a closet instead of a cupboard. My father had painted characters from fairy tales and children's stories on it: Willie Willie Winkie climbing up stairs with a candle on a stand, or Rip Van Winkle who slept against a large toadstool.

We were the only house in the neighbourhood to have pretty white picket fences. They did not last very long. In time, the rain seeped through the wood, damaging it, and the white paint cracked and turned grey like wrinkles on skin. They were soon replaced with a brick and mortar wall topped with iron spikes. At first it was just a brick wall, but the spikes were installed after Mr Roy was attacked outside. In this house my father did not have to bend before he entered, but I had to get on a stool to open the latch at the top of the door. The hallway in the front of the house had a display of frames on both sides of the wall. Each frame had old collector's stamps that had been methodically pasted on thick, cream-coloured paper. The stamps were ornate copies of paintings. Some had pictures of Napoleon and some were of orchids found in the Dutch East Indies. My father had made the frames himself. I watched as he drew line after line on pieces of timber, measuring before he would begin to cut and carve. He did it in the evenings after dinner under an inadequately bright tube light that flickered every few minutes. The floor was always littered with curly wood shavings, like clipped hair on the floor of a barber shop.

The front door was painted a rich mustard and the house a mix of chocolate brown and burgundy. We had a tin roof because, as my father explained to me, 'Meghalaya is an earthquake-prone area so a tin roof is the safest bet.'

Every time there was an earthquake, my father and I were always the first ones to wake up. 'Go, get your sister,' he would order me, but she would not wake up whenever I nudged her. He always ended up carrying her, still asleep, and I would follow at his heels, Bear in hand. The frames on the walls would shake and the floors would vibrate. My mother, quickly tumbling out of bed, would mutter, 'I think it's a small one. No need to panic,' although she always sounded unsure.

We would stand outside the house in the night, our nighties billowing in the wind, the stars shining, and when we felt there was no danger we would go back in. My mother complained, 'Uff it was a small one, no need to get so worried.'

My father shook his head and we would all crawl back into our warm covers.

We had a large backyard where we grew pumpkins, squash and maize. When it was the season for maize we planted them in three rows. They shot up like vegetative towers.

We hid between them when we played hide and seek. The pumpkins were small and green, but they were sweet and smelled very nice. My mother cooked them in beef stew, which was my favourite. They had large light green leaves and tendrils that curled around them. My father planted an orange tree; my mother said orange trees were proud plants that every garden needed, but apart from shooting up, it never bore any fruit, much to my disappointment. Near the water tank there was a bed of tiger lilies. They grew wild, like weeds, and we would trip on them when we were walking. I loved the orange and black pattern on their petals, but my mother made my father get rid of them after a while. She would flare up sometimes during one of her bad moments and make my father get rid of something. Sometimes it was flowers, another time a vacuum cleaner, one time a shirt I had. We always acquiesced.

There was a guava tree that always gave more guavas than we could eat. My mother used the excess guavas to make jam to give to family and friends. Winter always meant guava jelly and the smell of guava jam drifting in from the kitchen as my mother stirred the hot sticky mixture in its pot. We lathered it onto hot pieces of toast at teatime.

We also had a tree that sprouted sour tomato which my mother would use for her special pickles, and a plum tree. My father always wanted to pluck the fruit before the crows got to them. The crimson fruit, with its yellow fleshy insides, was bigger and sweeter than what you got in the Iew. He would feel sad when he saw half-eaten bits of fruit lying on the ground, with cavities where the birds had bitten into them.

I was loath to help my father pick plums because the tree's leaves were laden with caterpillars. We would take a sheet and my sister would hold one end and I the other. When we said 'Ready!' my father would shake the tree so the plums broke off from their flimsy branches. He shook and shook till they snapped off and fell onto our sheet. Sometimes a caterpillar fell along with the leaves and fruit; a spiny, shiny, curled up ball, untangling itself from the branches and leaves. I shrieked and let go of the sheet. My father, irritated, shouted, 'Don't act so silly! It can't hurt you.'

The ground floor of the house ran the length and breadth of the one above. My father placed a wall somewhere in the middle and cleaved the ground floor into two sections. Each was rented out to a small family. On the west side lived a family with their two sons. They came out to play with us in our backyard on the weekends. We played with marbles, digging small holes in the mud so we could knock them in. We carried our green marbles in a jar and would win or lose them during play. We tried to avoid earthworms as we dug through the mud. Bear sat on the side, monitoring us, as the soil kept getting on his soft, velvety coat. Sometimes we would take our kitchen sets to play. We would fill a cup with moist soil and gingerly turn it. What resulted was a perfectly smooth mound of mud in the shape of the cup. We took a minute to admire our work and then jump on the many mounds we had made, flattening them. Playing in the soil caused our nails to soften and break, and our skin to dry up and crack. 'Ni khynnah why must you always leh jaboh,' my mother shouted when she saw our muddy nails. To stop us, she bought a game of Chinese checkers for us to play with. 'Here, take this and share with Mynna and his brother.'

'Okay, but we will play with you first because you have to teach us,' my sister and I begged. Once we had learned we began to play with the two boys. We moved on to playing this every Sunday, competing with each other. Some days were spent exchanging WWF collectible cards with the scowling faces of famous wrestlers. We carried them in bundles tied with rubber bands, their edges worn and faces cracked from all the transactions.

On the other side of the ground floor house lived a man and his wife. I only knew him as Cousin Muscles, which is what my mother called him. This was in reference to Jerry's brawny cousin in a Tom and Jerry cartoon, whom my mother liked. I don't remember if he was anything like the beefy mouse. He had an Alsatian that we loved. The Alsatian only allowed my mother to put her whole hand in his mouth. We took him on walks sometimes when Cousin Muscles permitted us. He was too strong for me, so my father would hold the leash. We took him for a walk to the back of the colony where the milkmen stayed, where the air smelled like musty hay and cow dung. From the street, we could see their aluminium milk canisters, with their handles shining dully in the sun as they were laid out to dry. We loved dogs but we never kept one. 'I'll be the one who has to take care of him,' my mother would say.

Every evening we waited for our father to come home early from work so we could take Cousin Muscles' dog out. We were never told where his office was. 'He's gone to the forest,' was my mother's reply to all my questions about our father's work. Indeed, he would come home smelling of earth, his jacket dusty and his shoes caked with mud. His clothes would have nettles and briars clinging to them, as if they had hitched a ride from the forest. I would run toward him, and he would pick me up and put me on his shoulder, making me feel like a giant, my stomach doing a whoosh as he lifted me.

On some nights he would not come home till it was dinner time. On one such night, I could see deep furrows appear on my mother's forehead between her eyebrows. She looked worried, and I worried as a result. She stood near the gate with a lit cigarette, the chilly winds stinging her skin. My parents always smoked when they were anxious. At the end of every night, most ashtrays in the house were filled with ash. Mom made ashtrays of things that weren't meant to be ashtrays. On windy days the ash blew off the places my parents had stubbed cigarettes in, and I felt I was in a grey powdery snow globe. Unlike me, the stars above were indifferent to her worry, and the large tree we had in our garden rustled and shook, nodding in agreement, as the wind blew. In the distance we could hear a pressure cooker screech intermittently. There was a small frog that stayed in a flower pot in our garden. We called him Freddy. He croaked in the night whenever he thought we went too near. The light near our front door attracted insects, which were closely watched by the predatory lizards that clung to our brown walls. They stood silent, not moving, their tongues twitching. Giant moths tried entering the house as my mother absentmindedly always left the door open. I did not like them flitting about in the house, and I tried to throw them out. Their dusty gossamer wings struggled as I held them between my fingers and the powdery substance stained my fingers silver. 'Mom, close the door, bugs are starting to come in,' I shouted while I turned off the light in our porch.

'Oh yes,' she said absentmindedly. I was scared that the giant moths would come in and I knew I was not brave enough to catch those. My father had shown me one, a long time ago. He had called my sister and me, shouting from the bottom of the stairs, 'Ale! Ale! Come quickly and see this!' We had run excitedly to the backyard, and he had pointed at it. It was perched on a pillar and it had its wings closed. My father tapped it with his fingers to show me the pattern. When it relented to my father's gentle tapping and revealed itself to us, I was startled by its size and colour. It was as big as my face, its wings splashed with patterns of orange and red and black and white. The sides of the moth had patterns that looked like eyes. I was repulsed yet awed.

I stood next to my mother as she waited, on nights my father was late. 'You think a crocodile got papa?' I asked one night, as I placed Bear next to her for comfort.

'No, no. He is fine. He is just late. That's all,' she said as she tried to reassure me. We sat on the wicker chairs in our garden, and we waited in the dark by the light of the dying embers of my mother's cigarette. Finally, we heard the latch on the gate click, and I saw my father, dusty and tired, and I could feel him smile in the dark.

'Mom was worried because you are late,' I said as I went and stood next to him.

'Really?' he asked teasingly.

'Ni this child is just joking. I was perfectly fine,' she said slightly embarrassed but relieved as we walked back inside.

Behind ours were two other houses. In one lived a Bengali family and in the other, Assamese. We did not see each other very much because the entrance to their home was from the other side. We could see into their backyard because our house was at a height. The Assamese family would clean their utensils and clothes in their outdoor bathroom, and I would watch as the lady of the house threw yellow dish water down the drain. Tall bamboo trees hid the backyard of our Bengali neighbours so we never saw them.

One time there was a wedding function that was taking place in their home. It went on for seven days. It would start early in the morning and would go on late into the night. They caused such a din that on the sixth day, my father decided he had had enough. He started to throw stones from our house. 'Papa what are you doing?!' I asked, half surprised and half amused.

'These people just don't know when to stop,' he said; the way he said 'these people' sounding pejorative. Did he mean Hindus who blew on their conches, or dkhars who didn't worry about how much they might be disturbing their neighbours? I did not ask him to explain. 'They've been going on for seven days with no thought for anyone else. They need to know they're disturbing us,' he continued as he picked up more rocks.

He threw rock after rock just like how we would throw cold water at the stray cats when they would not stop howling in our yard while they were in heat. Just like it worked on the cats, the neighbours too eventually stopped.

--

Every year my sister and I looked forward to Christmas. We were always excited about the gifts Santa would get us. Even though year after year I received something new, Bear was always placed above them. One Christmas eve, when I was nine, my parents had guests over. They sat in the drawing room, near the fireplace, a few feet away from our Christmas tree. 'You get to bed early. You have to go to church tomorrow,' my mother said.

'But if you all are in the sitting room, how will Santa sneak in to put our gifts under the tree?' I whined.

'It's fine. He will leave them. Don't worry. Go sleep.'

I could not sleep. I was afraid that their presence would scare off Santa. I kept checking, peeking from the top of the stairs to see if the guests had gone. They had not. They poured glass after glass of wine as they laughed and talked loudly over each other. They finally left at two in the morning. When my parents had gone to bed, I snuck into the drawing room to check under the tree. I walked gingerly, trying not to wake them, but the cold floorboards creaked under my feet. As I had suspected, there were no gifts. I climbed back up the stairs, dejected, and continued to stay awake till the morning.

At eight in the morning, as soon as she was awake, my sister ran down the stairs. 'The fool,' I thought to myself as I brushed my teeth. She rushed back up soon and asked me, 'Aren't you going to go check yours?'

I looked at her, astonished as she held up her gifts, the wrapping paper dangling from the edge of a box of crayons where it had not been torn off properly. I ran downstairs and under the tree, I found two packaged items, sitting neatly with my name on them. 'Santa came through,' I thought.

I got a box of caramels and a hardbound children's illustrated book of the Mahabharata. In it I read the words: To D. Love, Santa. I was overjoyed. But soon after, I noticed that Santa's writing was similar to my mother's. When quizzed, she replied, 'Oh Santa can imitate anyone's handwriting.'

That answer satisfied me for a while. In later years, I started to suspect that my mother was behind the gifts. She signed all books this way. In other hardbound illustrated books she wrote, 'For my two suns', an inscription that she thought was funny because she had two daughters. I also began to think it was ridiculous that Santa only imitated my mother's handwriting. And although I soon solved the mystery of the handwriting, that Christmas was when my troubles with sleep first began. From then on, whenever I was very worried about something, I would not be able to sleep. Insomnia continues to plague me today and I often think of when it all started, on that cold Christmas night, standing by the stairs in my pyjamas and socks with Bear in my hands, worried for Santa.

—

As I grew older, I began to find that I did not need Bear as much as I once did. He was soon relegated to a musty corner of the room, safe in a plastic covering. In time that corner grew overcrowded. The video game set my grandmother got me for my tenth birthday joined Bear the following year and began to gather dust. The checkers board and the jar of marbles eventually joined them, as did the Casio keyboard I would practice my lessons on when I was eleven. Bear lay there among them, forgotten, until Buddy brought him out years later.

Buddy came to the house one autumn morning when we woke to the sound of gunshots. At first we were unsure about what to do, and my father went out to investigate. From our garden he saw police cars parked outside our neighbour Khongwir's house. Bah Khongwir lived in a house with an enormous silver gate, a little way down the road from where we lived. I had never seen him because he was always only in his car. My parents did not know the family very well because they kept to themselves, but I used to see Bah Khongwir's daughter Lorraine take their golden retriever out for a walk sometimes.

My father went to the Khongwirs' house and walked over to one of the policemen standing by the gate. Other curious neighbours had come to see what the commotion was about.

'What has happened?' he asked the policeman.

'Oh someone came in and tried to rob this house. They thought this family was still out on vacation.'

'How would they know that?'

'Tip shuh. They were surprised as hell when they saw the house was full and there was a big dog. Tried to shoot it. Ended up killing the owner.'

'Someone has died?!' my father asked, shocked.

'Yes, the husband. It's very sad. This kind of thing rarely happens.'

'What about the rest of the family?'

'Oh they're not wounded or anything. The burglars ran off.'

My father nodded and went in. As he later told us, Lorraine, on seeing my father, rushed toward him and said, with urgency in her voice, 'Take him,' handing my father the dog's leash. 'Take this dog with you. I can't worry about him now. I don't have the time to take care of him. I have to tend to my mother.'

'How can I take him?' My father said, astonished by such a request.

'Please help me. I really cannot be worried about this dog right now.' Lorraine had pleaded, tears still streaking cheeks.

My father felt sorry for Lorraine. She had just lost her father; he knew he had to help. He looked down at the dog, who seemed to understand that something terrible had happened. He was sitting down flat on the ground, quiet, his golden hair spread out on the floor. He was a beautiful golden retriever, and at that time there were very few people who had retrievers in Shillong. My father knew the dog was too expensive and precious to keep. He also knew that once everything was settled, the dog's owners would want him back.

'How about I keep him for a while. I'll come and give him back to you when you are ready to take him.'

'Yes! I can do that,' she replied, relieved to be handing him over.

'What's his name?' My father asked.

'Buddy,' she said her voice trailing off as she went into one of the rooms.

When we saw my father come in from the gate with a dog, my sister and I squealed with delight. A frothy, golden mop of a dog that was almost as big as my sister. My mother, surprised to see the creature, turned to my father, her eyes asking the question as though struck by aphasia. He related to my mother the tragedy that had struck the Khongwir household.

'Their house is like a fort. The wall is so high, and their gate is tough to jump over. How did they get in?' My mother asked.

'I have no idea. Everyone is in a panic in that house. Let's just keep this dog, and they will come pick him up after two weeks.'

'Okay, fine,' my mother said almost grudgingly.

Buddy the golden retriever stayed with us for two weeks. During that time, my sister and I kissed him goodbye every morning before school and ran back home as soon as we could so we could play with him. He sat and watched us eat in front of the TV every evening, salivating on the floor. We used him as a footstool, rubbing our feet against his soft fur. And although my mother hated to admit it, she loved the dog as much as we did. She spoiled him by feeding him mince meat from the butcher, which he would wolf down in seconds.

One day during those two weeks, I came home after school to Buddy chewing on my yellow bear. He had pulled Bear out from his corner in my room. The checkers board and keyboard were set askew, and the wires of the video game controllers were entangled.

'Buddy! Spit that out!' I shouted, yanking Bear from his mouth, tufts of fur falling through my fingers. 'How did you get him?!' I asked Buddy, as if he could answer. He put his tail between his legs and lay down on the floor next to me.

I looked at the damage he had caused. Bear's fur was full of holes around his neck, exposing the stuffing inside. One of his eyes dangled precariously on a piece of string like a spider from a web. I was distraught. My mother helped me stitch the eye back, and I sent Bear to the dry cleaners. He came back in time to comfort me, just as Buddy returned to his own home.

Once Buddy left us, I only saw him through the grille of that very large silver gate of the Khongwirs' house. I made it a point to always go to the gate to say hello to him when I walked home from school. His wet nose poked through the grille, and he always grew excited when he saw me. He always came out to the gate to greet me, until he stopped. He was not immortal like Bear.

When I was younger, I took Bear with me everywhere. I was superstitious as a child. I had 'lucky pyjamas', which I wore when I thought mom was angry with me. I thought those pyjamas would lessen the scoldings. I had lucky ties, lucky skirts. I used to carry Bear with me to school for luck. I felt that he protected me because on days I carried him with me, the older girl from tenth standard would not accost me. On days that I forgot to carry Bear, I would go running to my best friend, Yuva, because the tenth standard girl would always be waiting in hiding for me at break, to grab me and pinch me in my 'bathroom parts', as I used to call them. That only stopped when she left school, which was about the time I stopped carrying Bear with me.

I feared many things and believed these lucky objects served as a palliative to my anxieties. Bear was one such talisman, but Bear was also witness. He was with me when I had the chicken pox and the time I had been bitten by a stray dog. He was with me when I argued with my mother, and when I was having trouble sleeping. He was there with me when my mother was impatient with me during lessons, when I could not remember there was an eleven between ten and twelve. He was there with me when my father came home too late and the thunder rumbled angrily outside. He watched when my best friend left me.

Bear is still in my house. My mother would insist I throw him out but I always refused. I used to think that maybe our house had not been robbed on the night Bah Khongwir died because we had Bear in the house. I told my mother this, on the night that Buddy first came to stay with us. Incidents that bad rarely happened in quiet neighbourhoods like ours. That's what I thought at least, until one of the stray cats we used to feed had her back bludgeoned by a neighbour. We had to put her to sleep. I was very upset and cursed the monster who did that. What happened with our tenant several years later also made me question how well we knew our neighbours.

Back then, whenever Bear was at Mohandas's, the dry cleaners, I prayed extra hard that nothing bad happened while he was gone. It was always with relief that I went to Mohandas with the chit in my hand to pick up Bear. He always sat with the other toys behind the glass in the shop front. Years of getting him dry cleaned had caused him to fade. He, like all of us, aged. He still has the puncture wounds that were roughly sewn up by me, and his eye sits more securely on one side than the other. The rainbow on his paws have become discoloured and the pink of his nose has peeled off; it is now a dull milky white.

I did not take Bear with me when I left Shillong for college, there was never any space for him. He sits in a corner of my room, a relic of a time when I still worried about Santa, when we lathered guava jelly on toast on winter evenings, and I could still fit on my father's shoulders.

Mrs Trivedi

In the Hindi classroom one could hear Mrs Trivedi, 'Badi e ki matra, not chotti.' The class answered 'Yes, Miss' in unison, like clockwork.

No one understood nor bothered to ask why. Through listless eyes we watched her as she wrote vigorously on the board, breaking the chalk halfway before she finished her sentence. The floor was always littered with the broken halves that would soon be crushed under her feet. Powdered chalk caked the wooden floors. Her hair, her chin, her shoes would all be layered with white dust, as if she had just been baking. Her sonorous voice filled the room and intruded on our thoughts about lunch. The entire class waited for the sound of the bell that would signal the end of class. We invoked Ram Singh, the caretaker of the school, hoping he would manifest and walk past, bell in hand. We pricked our ears waiting for the class's death knell.

Mrs Trivedi could sense our distraction and she made

sure to mention there would be a spelling and dictation test for the chapter. 'Don't forget which story, girls. It's "Akbari Lota". Please take this test seriously. I don't want to see the same faces in this class.'

We all groaned, 'Yes, Miss.'

'The marks scored in this will be counted in the final exam at the end of the year, and you have to make sure you all pass.'

This announcement put a damper on our excitement, but we soon forgot about it once we were out of the classroom and playing with our friends. As the clock struck a quarter to twelve, we would see Ram Singh from a distance, upright and thin, his face resolved. Up and down he flicked his wrist, ringing the old ornate brass bell that had been in the school longer than he had. Clang clang clang.

Mrs Trivedi was a solitary creature. She never sat in the staff room where the other teachers had their lunch, exchanging gossip. She preferred to eat lunch alone in a quiet corner of the Hindi classroom, facing the wide windows along its left wall. Every day she took out a tiered tiffin from a red cloth bag that she kept in the cupboard. She removed tier after tier, laying them neatly in front of her. Gazing out of her window she began to eat, chewing thoughtfully with each morsel. When she was done she took a walk down the driveway that lead up to the school gate, cigarette in hand. This place was usually quiet, the ground wet from the rains and dew dripping from the row of eucalyptus trees that stood on one side of the road. The only sounds came from the residents of Lady Hydari Park, the school's neighbours. We used to see Mrs Trivedi mutter to herself as she walked, stopping every so often next to a eucalyptus tree to take in a deep breath, inhaling the sweet citrusy scent.

The girls in school liked to speculate about why Mrs Trivedi did not get along with the other teachers. We relied on hearsay and gossip to draw our own conclusions and weaved our own narratives. 'She's a divorcee! That's why she is so weird,' I had heard one of the girls conjecture.

'No, it's because she smokes so much,' another replied.

'How is that a valid reason?' I asked them.

'Well it's not very ladylike,' someone said.

I suspected that Mrs Trivedi's capricious behaviour drove people away. She was given to fits of anger which later accompanied a profound melancholia that affected all those within close range of her. No one understood why she behaved the way she did. On some days she was cheerful and funny, teasing and playful around us, but within hours she would be mumbling to herself as she scribbled angrily on the board. On days she was in one of her angry bouts, we knew to pay careful attention to our lessons.

I took Hindi as a second language option on the insistence of my mother, although I always had the option of taking Khasi, my native tongue. 'You will need to know how to read and write Hindi when you leave this town,' she said, with the surety only a mother would have. And so I studied Hindi, and was the only Khasi girl from my class who did.

Mrs Trivedi treated me well and was always attentive. I took extra tuition with her so I could get extra help with this language, so different to mine. Every afternoon when school was over, and everyone else had gone home, I stayed back so I could study my lessons with her. There were three other students from different grades who stayed back with me. It felt odd being at school after hours. The classrooms and the grounds were deserted, with only Ram Singh prowling the halls as he locked up.

The school I went to was established in the year 1900 when the British still ruled and Shillong was the capital of Assam. Half the school structures were old and built like Assam-type houses. Each classroom had wooden floors and wide windows which lacked the metal grilles otherwise ubiquitous in Shillong, making it easy for us to stick our heads and warn each other if we could see a teacher approaching. The older classrooms all had a fireplace tucked away in a corner, often one which had fallen into disrepair from not being in use. It was usually hidden away by a large abacus or a broken blackboard. In the kindergarten section of the school the abacus was used as a makeshift jail, and the little children were made to stand behind it to answer for their crimes. The ceilings were high, and the roof was covered in tin. In the monsoon months the rain would beat so hard against the roof that we could barely hear the teacher's voice over the raucous din. 'Miss, we cannot hear you! The rain is too loud!' One of us always quipped from the back.

'What rubbish!' The teacher dismissed us in an affected manner that would put any finishing school teacher to shame.

'Wait till it stops, Miss. Please!' We all joined in.

In the end she had to relent to our gentle but incessant prodding.

The school grounds had pine trees and weeping willows, eucalyptus trees and cherry blossoms, all lined up against the peripheral wall. Their presence caused strange caterpillars to fall on the ground: dark, horned and slimy. They stuck to walls, desks and chairs like they had been pasted on, defying physics. Near the basketball court there was a small brick sundial that had been placed there when the school was first built. Yuva, my best friend told me that there was a dead horse beneath the sundial. 'Those things sticking out aren't weeds but horse hairs,' she said, and for a long time, I believed her. There was an old hall and a new hall. The old hall was where we went to assemble each day to the tune of 'The Entertainer'. As soon as a teacher began playing, we were to march into the old hall. We gathered there to hear announcements, sing a song and say the Lord's Prayer. 'Our Father in Heaven...' We had memorized it. The new hall was for musical concerts which we held every alternate year. Most of the girls longed to be part of these musicals but only a few were chosen, with the teachers only picking their favourites. These traditions left behind a series of practices and mannerisms that failed to rub off long after we had left school.

The number of girls who needed and wanted an education swelled as the years passed and thus grew the need for building other structures, annexes and laboratories. The grounds behind the buildings were razed, and we then had another field to conduct our sports activities. The new buildings were cold, unfeeling structures that had nothing of the charm the old classrooms possessed. They were well-connected to the older structures, but they had no fireplaces. They were brick and mortar and they took in the swelling numbers with room to spare. They were functional, and that's why they were built. They did not have tin roofs, so none of the girls could complain they could not hear the lessons over the rain.

The Hindi room was smaller than the other rooms. It was an elective class, so there were fewer students here than in the compulsory classes. The room contained three rows of tables and benches, and an enormous table for the teacher. A large blackboard hung behind the teacher's desk. On one side there was a small cabinet in which Mrs Trivedi kept all her papers. A small cupboard stood in a corner on which she placed several Hindi books of literature. Here she sat the whole day as she took lessons intermittently. Here she sat while she waited for us to come to her for extra tuition. Here she sat when she mumbled to herself, stealthily smoking the one-off cigarette, trying to avoid being seen.

When she was in one of her better moods she would not teach us. 'Put the books away,' she would say, 'I don't feel like teaching today. Let's just chat.'

She could be quite scatter-brained, mixing up days of the week, forgetting that Wednesday was the day we stayed back for tuitions. She always came rushing back into class after realising too late. One time she actually forgot to come back. This was the day of the hail storm. A friend and I were sitting and waiting for her to come for lessons when we heard it, a loud great thud on the tin roof above our heads.

'What was that?' My friend said.

'I don't know, a cat?' I replied. Just as I said this, what followed was a series of loud thuds; it felt like we were being shelled.

'Oh god what is happening?'

We looked out the window to see giant rocks of ice, the size of footballs, falling from the sky.

'It's hail! But really big hailstones.'

'I've never seen them so big! Be careful, you might get hit on the head,' I said to her just as one broke through the glass door and fell on the teacher's table. I picked it up. It was cold and looked like icy white coral. As I held it, it was melting in my hand, the cold of the ice piercing through my skin.

'I told you the wind sounded spooky earlier! A storm was brewing. Look at this giant hail!'

'Quite scary. Let's just stay in till it dies down,' I said and we all nodded, watching the hail pound the muddied ground. The coral-like hailstones pelted the ground, shattering into smaller pieces. After half an hour of this onslaught, the skies cleared and it stopped raining. The ground outside was carpeted in hail. The ice on the grass looked like crystals that had been woven on green velvet. We had all but forgotten that we were supposed to be studying, and we soon began kicking the large hailstones like they were footballs. Some of the boarders came out of the hostels to play with us. The hostel girls usually never came down to play with us, but hail the size of coconuts was as good a reason as any to break tradition.

We had a great time that afternoon, but when I went home I saw that the hail had damaged several windows in my house. A few days after the storm, we heard that a boy had died because one of the hailstones had fallen squarely on his head.

Mrs Trivedi was distraught about the hailstorm. She had remembered that she had a tutoring class with us only when she had already reached her home. She did not have the numbers to our landlines and could not call to inquire if we had got home safely. The next day, she rushed to the assembly hall before assembly started and started looking for us in the lines. People thought it was strange to see her there because she usually never bothered to attend assembly. On seeing us, the furrows on her forehead smoothened and she heaved a sigh of relief.

'You girls are okay?' she asked softly.

'Why wouldn't we be?' I asked; my friend was taken aback by the question.

'I forgot we had a class that day,' she confessed sheepishly.

'Yes, we realized, but we stayed back till it was safe to come out.'

'Oh okay, that's good,' she said with finality and walked away.

For the next month she never forgot about the tuition classes, but after a while she began to miss them again.

—

'You girls should learn from D. Despite being a Khasi girl she has done better than you,' Mrs Trivedi said in Hindi class one day when I had scored the highest in a test. She lathered on praise whenever I did well.

'Oooooh,' the girls teased.

'I hope you begin to take lessons as seriously as she does.'

I slid down my seat, trying to hide as everyone threw me a look. I could hear them whisper 'teacher's pet' as the other girls nudged me.

'I'm not!' I said, embarrassed.

'Don't you have lunch together?' they asked, trying to put me on the spot.

I nodded noncommittally and brushed aside their questions. The truth was that I did have lunch with Mrs Trivedi. It was mostly because I thought she'd like the company. This was on days she did not go to the canteen to eat and when she had brought her own lunch. On those days I would take my tiffin to the Hindi room, and we would sit and have lunch together.

On one such occasion she asked me, 'What have you brought for lunch?'

'Atta,' I replied.

'What? You brought flour?' she asked in disbelief. She peered into my tiffin to see three rotis neatly packed. She laughed out loud exclaiming, 'These are rotis, and atta is the flour, beta!'

I did not know that I had said something wrong. I was twelve, and we called it atta at home. At least when we spoke in Khasi. It was only when I went home and told my mother what had transpired that she explained to me how I was wrong. I did not go and eat lunch with her after that because I felt ashamed. But she asked me to come back and I did, feeling silly for avoiding her. I had begun to encourage my friends to come have lunch with her as well. I enticed them with the thought of having the entire classroom to play in after she left for her walk. Eventually they came and saw that Mrs Trivedi was more at ease when she was having a nice lunch with us.

Sometimes Mrs Trivedi went on leave without informing us, and we were left to spend the class unmonitored. We were not eager to go back to the main classrooms to put ourselves under the ministrations of the headmistress, who took it upon herself to teach moral science during every free period.

The girls occupied their time playing games like Name, Place, Animal, Thing. We all drew straight lines on our sheets of paper to mark out even columns for each of those things. A letter of the alphabet would be chosen, and we each had one minute to think of something under each heading starting with that letter. The trick would be to think of obscure names, places, animals and things, because if you had the same words as the other players you would not get the full number of points. It made us work harder, to always be on the lookout for interesting names, poring over encyclopaedias, reading up about faraway places and strange animals, so one could quickly toss up a Quentin, Quetta,

Quokka and Quark if one had to and start the countdown. 'Tick tick one, tick tick two, tick tick three,' you would start as you saw the others sweat and suffer.

Of course, what was most fun, and most testing of even the strongest friendships, were the fights after each round about whether all the entries were valid. Whether 'Queeney' counted as a name because you had a cousin called that, or if a 'queen bee' counted as an animal or just someone trying to pass off a 'B' animal in a 'Q' row. I don't think I have ever played a game where we did all 26 letters because the game would always devolve into shouting and finger-pointing after only 9 or 10 letters, and fewer if we got a cursed Z or X early on.

As we got older, Name, Place, Animal, Thing gave way to other interests. Some girls sneaked in their mothers' *Elle* magazines, and we cut out pictures of Leonardo DiCaprio from them. We did the tests in *Cosmo* magazines about how to be better girlfriends, even though none of us had boyfriends. Our free periods were where I received any semblance of a sex education, with my classmates making jokes. The first time I learnt about masturbation was when Paarul, a classmate, had brought a magazine to school when we were in class seven. She immediately flipped to the advice column where people asked a 'sexpert' questions on sex and masturbation.

'What is this masturbation?' she asked us and we all shrugged. We did not know what it was and many of us did not care. But she would not let it go. 'I asked my dad but he did not tell me. It must be something he is too embarrassed to tell me.' Refusing to give in, Paarul then proceeded to take out a dictionary and read out to us what it meant.

'Yuck Paarul! Why do you have to tell us this?' One of us asked her, scandalized.

Paarul always seemed to know more about these things than us. One day when Mrs Trivedi had not showed up for class, she brought a magazine that had a short story written by Khushwant Singh. That name meant nothing to me before that day. We were all huddled at the back of the class as we read the story. It was story detailing a sexual act that, as we read the story to ourselves, made us screech, absolutely repulsed. Fiona snatched the magazine from Paarul and read the story out loud in front of the other girls. Paarul was horrified.

From then on, Paarul stopped bringing any magazines to class. She refused to take back the magazine she had brought, pretending she was never the one who brought it to school. The magazine ended up in the dusty old class seven library cabinet that stood outside the classroom, in the hallway. None of the teachers checked to see what was inside, and the rest of us were filled with glee, knowing it was there. Most of us at that school were inducted into the School of Know huddling over a magazine with a group of girls, looking up words we did not understand in the dictionary.

Our school shared a boundary wall with Lady Hydari Park, a misnomer if there ever was one because it was more than just a park. This park had animals, it had exotic birds, two bears, a few stags and a whole lot of monkeys. I remember seeing a clouded leopard on one visit, but I think he died soon after because the tree he would lounge on remained empty on my subsequent visits. The enclosure closest to us was the one that had stags, and we could see them grazing from some of the windows at school. And while there should have perhaps been a greater cause for concern that any one of our neighbours could leap over, or squeeze through the cracks in this wall, neither the establishment nor the parents expressed any concern. Still, sometimes the monkeys escaped and came to the school, standing on the fence, balancing themselves like trapeze artists about to roll onto the floor.

There was one time that a monkey got into the pantry of Kong C's makeshift canteen. Kong C was the lady who ran a small canteen inside the school grounds. She sold homemade food served in round tin plates for ten rupees. She had glass jars with candy shaped like slices of orange, and another jar that had the paan candy in its green and red wrapper. We always ate there if we forgot our lunch boxes at home.

On that warm summer day, as we were on our way to the canteen, my friend Yuva and I were startled to hear the agonized cries of Canteen Kong and Mrs Trivedi. We took off running towards the noise.

'Lah dep!' We heard Kong C shout, on reaching her stall.

'What happened?' I asked as I put my arms on my stomach, trying to catch my breath.

We found the Kong with a pan in her hand and Mrs Trivedi holding a ladle, trying to scare off a monkey that had managed to rifle through her things and find himself a tomato. She pointed at him to make sure we had seen him.

'What should we do?' we asked them frantically.

'Get Ram Singh,' Mrs Trivedi said through gritted teeth, perhaps afraid of agitating the monkey by speaking loudly. Kong Canteen nodded vigorously and silently.

Yuva ran off to get Ram Singh while I ran to the principal's office to tell her of the escapee.

Our principal—who was known for two things in particular, for putting on a British accent to sound more dignified and for maintaining her calm—almost tipped backward in her chair when I burst into her room to tell her about the escapee monkey running amok in the school grounds.

'Where did you say he was?' She said her voice raised, almost shrieking.

'With Mrs Trivedi and Kong C,' I replied.

'Right. Right. Let's go there and see this intruder.' She said, her voice shaky. She ran her hand over her silver bun touching the pins that held it to see if it was still in place.

'Someone has gone to get Ram Singh, ma'am. Maybe you should call someone from the zoo?' I suggested, seeing that the principal was merely feigning her composure and was at a complete loss.

'Quite right, child. That is just what I was about to do.' She offered a faint smile and proceeded to dial the number for the zoo.

The people at the zoo seemed remarkably unfazed that a resident of theirs had decided to take a jaunt in the girls' school next door. But they promised to send someone immediately on hearing the headmistress insist so vehemently on the other side of the phone. As we waited for them to arrive, Ram Singh took it upon himself to save the day and 'neutralize' the monkey. He lured the animal into one of the empty classrooms, placing food as bait. When the monkey went into the room, Ram Singh easily shut the door, trapping the monkey inside until the people from the zoo came to take him back. Ram Singh did all this with the same unperturbed expression that he wore when he would pick up a moth that had perched on a classmate's table.

Apart from the unfortunate tomato that was snatched before its time and the utensils that needed a second washing, monkey, Mrs Trivedi and Canteen Kong got off unscathed. It was going to be a little while before Mrs Trivedi went to get some pickle from the canteen, though. Someone from the zoo eventually came over and the monkey was returned to his home. We returned to our classrooms to eat whatever lunch was packed, sad to be missing Kong's dumplings as she went back to cleaning up the mess the unwanted patron had made in her establishment. The principal went back to her desk, fixed her hair and put her nose to her dusty files.

At the end of every school term came the final tests and the fear of being held back always loomed over us. What we scored on these tests would be counted towards our annual appraisal and we knew we had to do well. This fear was especially palpable during my time in the sixth standard. Two days before the Hindi terminal test we were in Mrs Trivedi's classroom, getting some last minute tutoring from her. She could not stay late that evening because she had a prior appointment, and she told us she would be leaving us half an hour early. She instructed us not to leave the school until our parents had come to pick us up. There was no telephone by which to contact our parents as this was after school hours, and we were forced to wait in the room till they arrived. When Mrs Trivedi left, we still had a half an hour before our parents would arrive to pick us up. We waited and talked, and played a game of Name, Place, Animal, Thing. Then when we grew tired of it, we talked some more.

Lucy told us that was worried she was going to fail. She put her head on the table and mumbled, 'I don't know what I'm going to do. I'm not following in class and all those words and idioms we have to memorize are making it really difficult for me.'

'It's fine, you'll do great,' I replied, trying to sound reassuring.

'Of course you would say that, you're the teacher's pet. You must have memorized things that are not even in the syllabus,' she scoffed.

'That's not true. I am not prepared for this exam. I haven't been paying enough attention to my lessons,' I said, shaking my head.

I really was not prepared that year. My parents had just got a cable connection, and all those new channels on television that I had not had access to before were enough for eleven-year-old me to get distracted. So I was equally worried.

Deishisha, the other girl in our class, was as unprepared as the two of us but seemed unfazed. She never worried about her test scores. She sat and listened to us as we fretted over the upcoming exam. Eventually she interrupted, 'If you're so worried about the Hindi exam why don't you just steal the question paper? It's right there in the cupboard. That is where Mrs Trivedi keeps all of them.'

She appeared cool and nonchalant as she said this. There was no trace of guilt on her face to show that she had said something almost sacrilegious.

'How can you even consider it, Deishisha?' I asked in a hushed tone.

'Yes, you know that we cannot do that,' Lucy replied. 'We would not get away with it.'

'That is not the only reason to worry about, Lucy. It's wrong to even consider that. That's cheating!' I said, positioning myself as the voice of reason and morality. 'Even if we fail it would be better.'

'But think about it. If you fail, your parents will know that you've been watching too much television. They might cut you off,' Lucy said insidiously as she raised her eyebrows.

We continued arguing, and I could feel my resolve waning. Lucy had a very good point. I was not ready to lose my television privileges so soon after having acquired cable television. In my young mind cheating was wrong, but I felt I was educating myself with all those new shows. I talked myself into it, reasoning that the look on my parents' faces on seeing me fail would be much worse than cheating. That perhaps the ends justified the means, that my parents would be none the worse for wear with this minor transgression and that my TV privileges would remain intact. My soul would mend itself over time. While having this internal monologue I decided that I would avoid church that weekend. I could not bear stealing, cheating and then lying about it in church.

But even while my mind went on this track, Lucy had already taken out a hair clip and was having a go at the small lock that was just one turn away from the damnation of my soul.

'No, don't do it. You'll be caught,' I said, hoping all the while they continued because I did not have the courage to go through with it myself. 'This is wrong. We're going to get caught. Ram Singh is going to come in and report us!'

The hollowness of my words rang in my ears. Deishisha frowned at me, and Lucy shushed me.

After many turns and clicks they finally unlocked it. It was a very small lock, the kind they used to lock suitcases. It was an easy task for Lucy who was adept at picking the lock of her mother's cupboard, which she did every other day for some loose change. I was made to stand and keep watch to ensure no one saw us. It was near impossible for anyone other than Ram Singh, who lived on the school premises, to catch us. During my vigil I managed to soak through my cardigan as I was sweating profusely from the stress of the heist. The other two, meanwhile, were trying to sort through all the question papers. There were question papers relating to classes three to ten, and rifling through them was turning out to be a challenge. After what felt like an eternity, they found the question paper.

'I found it!' Deishisha exclaimed gleefully as she waved the paper above her head triumphantly.

'Give it to me. Let me see it!' Lucy said as she tried to reach out for it. She managed to grab it and had begun to read it.

'I want to have a look as well. Share with us,' I said, and Deishisha nodded.

Lucy ignored us and continued to read.

'You know what, this is wrong.' I said, suddenly imbued with virtue, 'Give it to me, and I'll tear it. We will pretend this never happened and just do the exam as is.'

I don't know at that time if this was because I felt that what we had done was wrong or whether I was afraid that Lucy would not share. All I knew was that I was overcome by a strong desire to tear that piece of paper. I reached out for it and once I had it in my hands I made a cursory glance: 'Write a letter to your uncle...' and it trailed off because before I knew it, there was another set of hands that had grabbed the other edge of the paper. It was Lucy and she wanted the paper back.

'I'm not done reading!' she exclaimed. Deishisha sat on the side watching all this, unperturbed.

Lucy was perfectly able to read with my hands on the other edge of the paper. 'Look there are no questions from

"Pratiksha"! But she made us study that!' She screeched. I looked at where she was pointing and just as I did I felt much like Lady Macbeth and wanted nothing but to get rid of the incriminating document that was in my hand. It was proof to how I had gone against what I was taught at home. I wanted to wash this crime off my hands and before Lucy could stop me, I had grabbed it from her and tore it in half.

As if in retaliation, Lucy took the pieces from me and tore them even further until there was nothing left but six small pieces of paper. She took advantage of my shock to stuff the scraps into her bag and that was that. We no longer discussed it. Our parents arrived and we pretended we had forgotten about what we had done. All the same, Deishisha had the good sense to lock the cupboard on our way out.

The next day the whole class waited outside the examination hall for the bell to ring, signalling the beginning of the exam. We may not have been prepared with our lessons, but we came prepared with the right amount of stationery. We all stood there with our pencils, ink pots, rulers, and ink pens. We held our exam boards to our chests as though they were shields in the battle arena we would now be entering. We knew that our shields needed to reflect our personalities, so some were coloured and some were printed with our favourite cartoon characters. It was some time before I could afford the pale lilac one I got much later that year. For now it was a dull, brown cardboard adorned with stickers.

Just as we were stepping in I saw Lucy cowered in a corner reading from her backpack. I snuck up behind her, looked over her shoulder and found her reading the pieces of the paper we had torn up the day before. She had taped them together.

'You did not throw it? You sly girl!'

'Keep quiet and come here and read this with me,' she said throwing me a dirty look.

I went and sat down beside her 'You wrote the answers also! You could have shared with us!'

'There's no time! Read now, be angry later.' We held the paper protectively making sure it was not fully out of the bag, holding it tight.

The final bell rang, and we went in, shields in hand. When the results came out I found that I had passed and managed to keep my TV privileges intact. Lucy had surprised everyone, especially Mrs Trivedi.

'Lucy has surpassed all expectations. From failing to scoring the highest! Let this be proof that hard work pays off.'

She started to pay special attention to Lucy from then on, much to Lucy's displeasure.

Days after the exam, as we were having our lunch Mrs Trivedi commented, 'The lock does not snap as well as it did. I wonder why.'

I felt a stab of panic and kept my nose buried in my lunch box.

—

Near the end of the school term everyone had grown accustomed to Mrs Trivedi's eccentric ways. Although her mood swings were difficult to deal with, when she was having one of her better days the girls could see she was a good sort. She did not play favourites or meddle with the girls. She neither indulged in gossip nor did she pit any of the students against each other, which was more than you could say about many teachers in the school. Mrs Trivedi didn't care what an important personage your father was or how much money your parents had. When she was angry, she was angry with everyone, and when she was pleasant, she was nice to all. She was especially attentive to the non-Hindi speaking girls such as myself and Lucy, because she knew we had a harder time of it.

I was welcome to sit in her classroom anytime I wanted. Some days I sat there by myself when I had had a fight with my friends, or if I had done badly in class, and I wanted to be alone. Mrs Trivedi never minded. In return for this special treatment, and later perhaps to assuage my guilt over the incident with the exam paper, I kept her room neat. I dusted the blackboard, her chairs and tables. I arranged the books neatly and sometimes convinced Ram Singh to give me some fresh flowers to put in the empty vase that stood on the bookshelf, gathering dust. Someone had gifted it to her on Teacher's Day.

One afternoon soon after I had just turned thirteen, I took solace in the empty Hindi room. I was upset that Yuva and my cousin, who was younger than me, had already gotten their period, but I had not. I felt they had achieved something which I had not.

'It came,' Yuva had told me one morning during the assembly.

'What are you talking about?' I asked her.

'Oh you know, the thing everyone is getting. The thing Deishisha got first,' she said, embarrassed.

'Oh you got your P?!' I whispered into her ear.

Yuva nodded. I think my face fell because she then immediately said, 'I am sure you will get yours soon'.

Before she could say anything else, I could hear Chopin playing inside the assembly hall, saving me from having to feel worse about myself with her looking at me.

That entire day I avoided my friends. Yuva had been inducted into the unspoken adult girl club, and I was watching from the periphery. I went to the Hindi classroom during the lunch break to distract myself and started cleaning. Mrs Trivedi came in and saw me beating the dusters a little too hard against the wall.

'Arey why are you being so aggressive with that duster?' she asked.

Embarrassed, I kept the duster aside and muttered, 'Sorry Miss'.

'You seem bothered by something,' she said watching my face as I averted my eyes.

'No, nothing Miss.'

'Tell me! Come, come. Get it off your chest.'

I kept quiet and smiled sheepishly. I knew discussing periods with a teacher was something quite out of the ordinary. Even in an all girls' school, the girls and the teachers were very prudish about things like menstruation. Every time a stray dog dragged out a used sanitary napkin from the bathrooms, all the girls acted horrified and ignorant at the same time, as if they did not know what a sanitary napkin was. Our biology lesson on menstruation and sexual reproduction taught us nothing, as the biology teacher skipped a couple of crucial paragraphs. None of us noticed as we languished in our hard seats, hypnotized by her voice. Everything my classmates and I learnt about sex, we learnt from the worn out Sidney Sheldon and Danielle Steele novels we borrowed from the U Like lending library tucked away in a small corner in Laitumkhrah, and, of course, from Paarul's Khushwant Singh story.

'Come come, we are good friends, I think. You can confide in me,' Mrs Trivedi said encouragingly that day as she poured me some warm tea inside the cap of her flask. She then poured herself some in the giant mug she drank out of. 'World's Best Wife', it read.

I hesitated before I began. I was not used to telling adults how I felt. If I was sad I usually ran to Yuva to feel better, but this time I could not.

Outside, everyone was enjoying their lunch break. It was very windy and pine cones broke from their branches and fell to the ground. The girls picked them up and threw them at each other playfully, squealing if they got hit. In March the wind was always strong and dry. Mrs Trivedi began to shut the windows as the papers on her table began to fall on the ground. She was wearing a nice purple saree, I noticed. She usually wore sarees when she was in a good mood.

She came up and sat in front of me, not saying a word, waiting for me to tell her what was bothering me. Sitting in silence was far more painful, and eventually I began to talk.

'Nothing, Miss, just that everyone is ahead of me, and I feel like I have been left behind.'

'What do you mean?'

'Oh it's just that I have not got my P yet, Miss,' I said, my face flushing.

'Is that all?' Mrs Trivedi said calmly as she sipped her tea. She kept quiet for a second as if forming the sentence in her head before saying anything. 'Do not worry. You will get it soon. I got mine a few months after my thirteenth birthday. You just turned thirteen. Wait a month or two,' she smiled reassuringly.

'But Miss, Yuva got hers before her birthday! How come?'

'Oh that happens. There is nothing wrong with you. Trust me. You have your chai and go sit with your friends. You just have to be patient.' She then told me about the time she got her period for the first time, and how she thought she was dying. 'My mother explained to me that it was a good thing and also that I wasn't dying,' she said. 'I told her not to tell anyone but I think she told my father.'

It helped ease my worry, listening to Mrs Trivedi tell me about her experiences as a teenager. We even laughed together. It felt strange connecting with her on such a topic, and to be spending my lunch break with a teacher. It was considered an aberration or a waste by my friends. But I did not think I could talk to another adult in the manner I did with her that day. She made me feel comfortable and did not talk down to me. I sat with her until I saw Ram Singh walk past with the bell signalling the end of the break.

Mrs Trivedi never mentioned our conversation again, and I was glad for it. I started to pay more attention to my Hindi so she would be proud of me.

When the windy March weather was replaced by the monsoon, Mrs Trivedi began to miss classes more often. When she was in class she taught us hurriedly, skimming quickly through chapters just so we could finish our course. She was still kind and warm with me, but we never had heartfelt conversations like we did earlier. Some of us chalked it down to her having a fight with one of the teachers. We had seen her shout at one of the English teachers recently. I thought it was because Lucy had asked her once in front of the whole class if she was married or not. Mrs Trivedi had become very quiet after that.

That year after the Durga Puja holidays, when the air was starting to get chilly and the cherry blossoms had begun to dot our skyline, we got a new Hindi teacher. She was standing there in our classroom one day, cleaning the blackboard, her back to us. She was young and seemed eager as well as intimidated by the class of young girls. She told us she would not be starting any new lessons as the year was over but she looked forward to teaching us the next year. We were very curious about the new teacher and could not help wondering where Mrs Trivedi was.

'Where is Mrs Trivedi? Is she no longer our teacher?' Lucy asked her.

'Oh Mrs Trivedi will no longer be teaching you. I'll be the new Hindi teacher. My name is Mrs Bhardwaj,' she smiled and said.

Teachers in government schools rarely ever quit. The pay was much above that of a private school teacher. The process of removing a teacher who is part of the permanent staff of a government school was a very cumbersome and long one. We all deduced that Mrs Trivedi must have left of her own accord.

'Where did she go? Has something happened to her?' someone quipped from the back.

'I'm new here, and I don't really know, but I'm told she has gone back to her hometown.'

Out of loyalty to Mrs Trivedi I decided that I would not like the new teacher. She was a half-Khasi, half-dkhar woman who seemed phlegmatic in comparison to the choleric Mrs Trivedi. She never looked out of the window wistfully and never skipped a class. She was always on time, and she stayed with her husband. She never smoked. She was also not as attentive to me as Mrs Trivedi, and I soon started failing. I then had to take extra tuition classes with another teacher, Miss Sumitra, every Monday, Wednesday and Friday after school.

No one knew why Mrs Trivedi left. Some said she was back with her husband in Kanpur and that they had made amends. Many joked that she had finally been institutionalized. But soon people forgot about her. Everyone moved on to the next thing, the next piece of gossip, the next monkey escape.

Before that happened, I managed to get her number in Kanpur from one of the teachers. Some of my classmates and I called her from the landline in the teacher's common room once during our lunch break. She was happy to hear from us. We could not talk to her for too long because it was a long-distance call and the 'tch tch' from the other teachers was distracting. The line was not very clear and the static over the phone reminded me of just how far away she must be. I struggled to hear her, but we stretched the conversation as best we could, until the distant rings of Ram Singh's bell told us it was time to hang up the phone and let go.

Mr Sarkar

I failed mathematics my first term in the eighth standard. My parents did not take it well. For a while after, my mother would sit with me every day after school and tutor me. On chilly evenings when it was beginning to grow dark, I came back home from school to my mother waiting in the dining room with a notebook and a cup of tea. At about that time in the evening, my father started closing our large windows to make sure the mosquitoes did not get in. In the drawing room my sister drew the curtains. There was silence in the house because my mother drove away my sister and father after they were done closing up the windows. It would get so quiet that the only thing you could hear was the sound of crickets in our backyard and the conch being blown in the colony behind ours, signalling prayers.

I hated those evenings. 'Sngewthuh ne em?' My mother asked me to make sure I understood because my face gave away nothing. I did not want to tell her that I had not understood and nodded vigorously at regular intervals so she felt assured.

All our tutoring sessions together did was make me more scared of mathematics. My mother lacked the patience to teach me and I, the inclination to learn. It thus fell upon me to find a tutor who my parents could pay to take lessons. Someone who would not be as infuriated by my inability to comprehend quadratic equations as my mother was.

My search for a tutor took me first to the new mathematics teacher, Miss Sarkar, who had begun teaching us that year. She was soft-spoken and patient, and I thought it would be best to learn from her. With much trepidation I slunk up to the front of the class one day, stood next to her table, leaning against it for support and said, 'Miss,' barely hearing the sound of my own voice. 'Would it be possible to take tuitions with you after school?' I asked, swallowing my words in a way my father hated.

'Oh, I can't, dear,' she smiled and said, 'It's just not possible. There are already too many girls I have to teach. My hands are full.' Miss Sarkar looked sympathetically at me. On seeing my face fall, she added, 'Why don't you go to my father? He is a retired maths professor and he also tutors.'

Reluctant though I was, not knowing who and what kind of teacher Miss Sarkar's father was, I took her suggestion to my parents. 'You can go for a month and see how it goes,' my father said to me. 'He may be good and if he isn't, we can look for another tutor.'

Anything was better than sitting every evening with my mother, trying her patience. That is how I began to go to Mr Sarkar's house for lessons.

Mr Sarkar lived in Laban. I always walked there after school with my friends who were also taking tuitions with him. We had to go three times a week. We took the scenic route through a path that no cars could go through because it was too narrow, where the Um Shirpi ran alongside and under us. It garbled beneath the bridge under our feet, frothing around the plastic bags that had been discarded into it. This river and the Wah Umkhrah cut through the city and joined each other in Umiam Lake. The Wah Umkhrah was said to be divine. These two snaked through the city, reminding me of the great serpent Jormungandr who surrounded the earth, from the Norse stories my father read to me from his prized hardbound collections.

Laban was on an incline, and it was tough to walk up the sloping, winding road, our bags laden with books. However, we enjoyed our walk there; it gave us time to fill each other in on the gossip we had amassed in school. The path had homes on either side that were fenced by crude hollow bamboo sticks overgrown with ferns or creepers. There was the one odd house with a brick wall perimeter crowned with barbed wire to keep out burglars. We had a fixed routine: a muffin from Hot Cross Buns Bakery, which was along the way, and we each bought a packet of chips to share during the lesson. Also on our route was a boys' school and when we passed it the girls pretended they were not eyeing the building, even while darting glances at the gate.

On days when it rained my grandmother would send her car to drop me to Mr Sarkar's house, but I much preferred it when we walked. When we were done early at Mr Sarkar's, my friend Poonam and I would go back to hers, have tea and gossip. She lived close to Mr Sarkar's and would invite me over often. She possessed something rare that very few of us had in 2000: a working dial-up internet connection. The first thing she did when entering her room was turn the router on, a screeching sound filling the air, and the room glowed a cool blue. She sat on her swivel chair and typed in 'shaadi.com'; we waited a few minutes and when faces sprang on the monitor, we scrolled through the profiles one by one and laughed while drinking tea with bourbon biscuits. It always got too dark by the time we were done and out of worry my grandmother would send her car to pick me up. My home was at the other end of town.

Mr Sarkar lived in a two-storey house. Next to the house, on its left, was the annexe where he tutored us. There were two rooms, one for the boys to sit in and one for the girls. It was imperative to him that the boys and the girls were separated. He did not want us to get distracted from our lessons.

The rooms had long wooden tables and chairs. In the rainy months it always smelled damp, the walls and furniture reeking like a wet dog. We always kept the windows open, or the smell would mingle with that of the dumplings the boys were fond of eating in the classroom. Sometimes in those wet months we would come to the class with our uniforms soaked and wait for our skirts to dry before we sat down on the benches. The boys had no reservations about taking off their shoes to dry them out, filling the humid air with the putrid smell of their sweaty socks. The smell carried over to our room. The boys' room did not have enough windows, and they had to make do with the ersatz light from the bulbs above their heads.

The boys always found a way to circumvent Mr Sarkar's attempts at segregation. It was pointless however because none of the girls considered them attractive. There were only two of them at the beginning, and they always sat too close to each other. One was slight and swarthy with a high-pitched voice. He wore glasses and always seemed pleased with himself as if he had just told a witty joke. The other was stocky and hairy. He had a wispy moustache that he refused to shave, which reminded me of the small hairy caterpillars that perched on my mother's chrysanthemums. Their names were Partha and Sudeep, and we called them Peepee and Susu.

Outside the annexe was a small path next to which Mr Sarkar had planted sweet peas on a moist bed of soil. A grille that came up to the knees separated Mr Sarkar's home from the building next door. The girls, much to their delight, soon found out that the neighbouring house was a boys' hostel. Some of them began to wait outside in full view of the hostel after having hitched their skirts higher than what was permitted in school. They did this before lessons started and made sure Mr Sarkar never saw them. They always pretended they were talking about lessons and ignored the boys who came in and out of the hostel. The boys never pretended, smiling as they called out to the girls. Sometimes they even came to the fence and spoke to us.

Tuitions began at four o'clock and were done by half past five, and in that time Mr Sarkar taught us everything he had to. He was methodical, concise, spoke softly and never raised his voice, always patient with all of us. A distinguished-looking man of fifty, Mr Sarkar had a full head of hair that had completely turned white. He also was very tall, standing at almost six feet, strong and well-built. I heard that he had been popular among women when he was a young man. His wife was a Khasi woman who had married him on the condition that he convert to Christianity. She would come to the tuition room occasionally to offer us some tea and cake. She wore pretty pastel jaiñsems and always had her hair up in a tight bun. She carried an air of solemnity with her when she came to the room, but always smiled when we spoke to her, and was attentive to Mr Sarkar. They had raised both their children Christian.

Although I was terrible at maths, Mr Sarkar tried hard to help me improve. He knew that some of the others, who came to him just for a little assistance, were better at maths and would do just fine with the amount of time he spent teaching them. He played to people's strengths, giving each one only what they required. He saw my reticence as politeness and good behaviour. When some of the girls would be done with their sums before the rest of us, they would start talking loudly, trying his patience.

'Why can't you be silent. You cluck like hens. Can you not see the others have not finished? You should learn to be quiet and ladylike, like D,' he said every so often.

I would get very embarrassed each time. I did not understand why being quiet was a good thing. I heard this from Mrs Trivedi, and it would be reiterated by Mr Sarkar. He did not know that when his back was turned, I would participate in conversations with the other girls as well.

Still, in the first terminal test that came after we had started going to him for tuitions, I passed my mathematics paper. I did not score well, but I passed, and because of this I continued to go to him. We all went to him the afternoon of the results to tell him how we had scored.

'So girls, tell me how you fared?' He asked.

As expected, Ishita, the school topper, had scored well, and she said triumphantly, 'Sir, I scored a 93.'

'Good, good,' he dismissed. 'And you?' He turned to me.

'Sir, I did not do so well,' I said, slightly embarrassed. I told him the meagre score I got and he was elated.

'That is very good! I am sure you will do better than that next time,' he said, patting me on the back.

I did not think he was being patronising because he was never disingenuous with us. He truly believed I had done a good job. From failing I had managed to score marks that, although not a 93, were good enough. He knew that all he had to do was help me overcome my irrational fear of the subject.

—

As time went on, I began to notice that on Saturdays when we had tuitions there were some girls who were asked to come earlier than the rest of us. While the Khasi girls were called for tuitions at eleven o'clock, the others were asked to come at half past ten. I was worried that Mr Sarkar had begun to have favourites and only called them for tea and cakes to his house. I knew they had tea and cakes because these girls did not want to come have chaat and icies with us after class. It had become a ritual of ours to eat some aloo muri chaat, which we washed down with icies on our way home. An aloo muri vendor sold and prepared it on the roadside, standing with his foldable wooden table, mixing up his ingredients. We could see him from afar, his bright green table with its glass compartments which glinted in the sun. Each compartment was filled with puffed rice, grams and small round puris.

'Bhaiyya give for five rupees mo,' Lucy asked him when she went to buy some, holding up a worn-out note. Five rupees would go a long way, and it was enough to fill our stomachs and spoil our dinners.

'Theek hai,' he replied as he lifted the lid from the tiny glass compartment and placed a handful of puffed rice in a mixing bowl. He cut up the potatoes that he kept in a small plastic bag, chopped up onions which crunched with each slice, and sprinkled the mixture with a spoonful of spices. The cumin powder got in our noses, and our mouths would salivate at the smell of the tamarind water that he would pour into the mixture with his big wooden ladle.

'Mama iai shuh seh,' we coaxed, asking for more tamarind water.

He replied in broken Khasi, 'Ni thait! Toh toh', he acquiesced and grudgingly gave us a spoon.

It was sour and spicy, burning in our throats as it went all the way down to our stomachs, and we all loved it. He mixed all these ingredients with the finesse of a chef, funnelling it into a paper cone that he had made out of a piece of paper he had torn out of an old school book. He carried this entire table and all the ingredients to his spot daily. We all loved talking to him as he made our share and doled it out in paper cones. We communicated in a creolized language of Khasi, English and Hindi.

'Te you don't feel cold standing out here in the winter?' I asked once.

'Leh kumno, I have no choice, I have to feed my family. I also have to send back money to my hometown. My mother lives with my sister.'

'Oh kumta. Is that what you have to do? Te when do you go to visit her?'

'When all of you have winter holidays. During Christmas time. Business is slow then.'

'Oh haoid kein. But come back in January mo. That time the class ten kids are preparing for boards em, and we have to go for tuition and we feel hungry.'

He chuckled and said, 'Yes I will come back by then'.

When we were done with our small talk we took our little cones and toothpicks with which we picked up the little bits of potato, and waved goodbye to him as we walked home. I tried to be more polite with the aloo muri men especially after I saw some local boys rough up one outside the park. Sometimes these men, being mostly dkhar, would have a hard time with the local Khasi boys who refused to pay after they had given their chaat. But the aloo muri men never left, brushing off each altercation with the locals, carrying their foldable tables to their spots, trying not to spill the tamarind water.

When the girls kept going to Mr Sarkar's house earlier than some of us, my curiosity grew, and I felt the need to investigate. If I was being honest with myself, I knew that I had begun to feel left out. I was very fond of Mr Sarkar, and I did not like that he was not inviting me to his brunches. It also struck me that it was only the dkhar girls who were being called early. So on a cold Saturday morning in October I told my parents that Mr Sarkar was teaching us for an extra hour that day and went in early. Outside his house I met Poonam, who was surprised to see me.

'What are you doing here?' she asked, raising her eyebrows.

'Why? I was invited. Sir called me at the last minute and told me to come early,' I replied, trying to sound convincing.

Poonam looked perplexed. 'But are you sure? I don't think you need this.'

I had no idea what she meant and insisted that I had to be there.

The other girls seemed surprised on seeing me as well. 'You better wait in the tuition room if you know what's good for you,' someone said, smiling slyly.

I ignored her and filtered into Mr Sarkar's house with the rest of the girls. As soon as I entered my eyes had to adjust to the colour of the room. The walls were a bright pink and the sofa a dull orange. It was an adequately sized room, with thick mauve drapes that blocked the light. On the wall opposite the door there hung a huge imitation print of *The Last Supper* that had been framed tastefully. The chairs in the living room all pointed in the direction of the television that stood on the west side of the room. In one corner of the room there were cabinets with sliding doors. It seemed to contain the most varied set of items, from fancy crockery to old soft toys that Mr Sarkar's children must have played with when they were younger. The room was spotless. There was no sign of dust, and the tiled floors sparkled letting off a faint smell of lemon.

We all proceeded to the chairs that sunk as we sat, making us move forward to the edge to get comfortable. I sat in the corner, hoping I would go unnoticed. Mrs Sarkar entered with the maid and laid out some tea, cakes and a copy of the Bible on the coffee table in front of us. As she turned, Mrs Sarkar saw me and asked, 'Oh D, why have you come?'

'Oh aunty, I came early so I thought I'd just tag along,' I said nervously.

'That's good. Even for believers it is a good thing to attend,' she said, giving me a smile.

I was slightly startled and thought this was an odd thing to say. The other girls seemed unfazed and proceeded to drink tea and eat cake. After five minutes of waiting, Mr Sarkar walked into the room. He said nothing to me but only nodded and welcomed all the girls.

'Your presence here is proof of how the younger

generation will be making the world a better place,' he said with the solemnity of a priest. 'Let us begin.'

Mr Sarkar sat on the one empty seat close to the television and soon his wife joined him. He turned on the television with a remote and I saw, through the corner of my eyes, the other girls starting to get restless.

What he played for us on the television was something that I would never have guessed. A series of videos, each bleaker and more tragic than the last one. They were on the perils of hell and how non-believers or 'heathens' were damning themselves to an eternity of fire and brimstone.

'Repent!' A man in one of the videos barked at us, the veins on his forehead throbbing. He exhorted the watchers of the video to turn away from evil ways and to accept Christianity as the one true religion.

Mr and Mrs Sarkar sat on their seats, their faces alternating between composed and encouraging as they nodded along with the man on the television. The girls all had their arms folded, some of them suppressing a grin and many of them just rolling their eyes. I was stupefied by the entire thing.

After what felt like an eternity, Mr Sarkar switched off the television. Mrs Sarkar started handing out pamphlets she took out from her Bible. They were colourful and innocuous-looking, but on reading you realized they described the perils of hell. They had pictures of smiling children, saved from damnation.

When this entire bizarre exercise was over, we all walked out of the house quietly, our eyes squinting as we adjusted to the sunlight. When we were a safe distance from Mr Sarkar's, the other girls burst out laughing on seeing my face. 'We told you not to come,' Poonam said as she slapped me on the back playfully.

'Is this what he does? Talk to you about hell?' I asked.

'Yes!' They said in unison.

'But why?' I cried out, almost whining.

'Because he thinks he needs to save us and genuinely believes we need saving,' Devika, a classmate, replied as she sat down next to me.

'Why do you go then?' I asked with my eyes narrowed.

'We go because he's a nice man, and we don't want to offend him. We also go because this is a ten-minute session, and the cake is really nice. The biggest reason is that he is a damn good mathematics teacher, and we cannot afford to start looking for a new one just because this one has quirks,' Poonam said with an air of finality.

'Is this why he does not invite the Khasi girls? All this while I thought he did not like us, and he was playing favourites,' I said laughing out loud as I said it.

'Well you're lucky you don't have to be saved,' Poonam teased.

I began to see everything in a new light. The way Mr Sarkar spoke to us. How his daughter came to the tuition room and prayed with us sometimes. She never wore any makeup and always dressed modestly, which I had chalked up to her being plain. Even Mrs Trivedi wore very little makeup and was almost dowdy, but I had dismissed it as a dkhar thing. But now the crosses in our tuition room and the paintings in Mr Sarkar's home all made more sense. I thought that Mr Sarkar, like other converts who I had seen in my church, eventually became more devout than those who started off Christian.

I tried to learn more and found out that Mrs Sarkar was a devout Pentecostal Christian, and Mr Sarkar was the same. As a Presbyterian Christian, I did not know what a

Pentecostal was. I asked a friend of mine, who told me, 'The Pentecostals think the Pope is the devil. Don't believe me, but those Pentecostals are weird. They believe all sorts of strange things.'

This was an unsurprising statement to hear in Shillong, where one sect of Christians always had something silly to say about another. Some said the Church of God Christians were very puritanical, others thought that the Pentecostals were odd. The Baptists were one way, the Presbyterians were another, and they all disliked each other, thinking theirs was the best method of worship. Nonetheless all were united in their disdain for Roman Catholics. Although their mutual dislike never led to anything but snide insults delivered over tea, it sometimes happened that two people from differing sects would not marry unless the other converted. I thought this odd as the deity to be worshipped was the same, only the manner would be different. 'They are all Christians,' I would yell exasperatedly whenever I would hear of such a thing. As far as I knew, Miss Sarkar never married, and I often wondered if this was the sort of reason why.

We all continued to go to Mr Sarkar till we were in the tenth standard, up until our board exams. He was able to deliver on his promise of helping me pass although it was with a slightly embarrassed shuffle that I entered his house and told him my very low marks. He continued to be encouraging and kind. He wished us all luck on the day I last saw him, when we went to him with our board exam results.

I never forgot Mr Sarkar, but as I grew older I never found the time to stay in touch or visit him. I did ask my friend Poonam, who was his neighbour, about him whenever we got to talking on the phone and there was a lull in our conversation.

Years later, when I had finished college, during one such conversation with Poonam, I found out that Mr Sarkar had passed away after a protracted illness. He had had cancer.

Poonam told me she had gone to see him in the hospital. 'He refused to take any medication and was against chemo,' she said.

'Why though?' I asked, quietly.

'He felt that he deserved to be sick and, that perhaps it was God's will or that he was being punished. Either way he said this was all part of God's plan,' she said dejectedly.

'That's ridiculous.'

We were silent on the line for some time. 'You remember Miss Sarkar?' Poonam said eventually. 'She was there. She's become hep now.' She giggled slightly.

'What do you mean?'

'Oh just that she wears jeans now. When I saw her, she was wearing lipstick and had a pixie haircut. Also she's become an atheist and was very upset with her father's refusal of treatment.'

'Wow, a lot has changed.' I thought back to the last time I had seen Mr Sarkar, at the end of tenth standard when I had gone to tell him about my ICSE exam results. He stood at the doorway and shook my hand vigorously, pleased that I had passed.

'That's terrible that he passed away, though. I wish I had known. I would have gone to visit. I was fond of him.'

'We all were. I hope he found the peace he promised us,' Poonam said.

'I hope so too,' I replied, my voice trailing off.

The Lawmali Graveyard

He lay in the cool, wet earth. The laterite soil under our feet was always cold or wet, and sometimes both, because it never stopped raining, and it never got too warm. We remembered my grandfather every December when we had to lay flowers on his grave. He died on 17 December 1984, and each year since then my family paid a visit to Lawmali Graveyard on that date. During the week leading up to the day we busied ourselves in preparation for the visit. Up until the time I left my home to go to college I was very involved in the entire preparation. As the eldest and thereby de facto head of my cousins, it was my duty to see to the collection of flowers, ferns and pliable twigs for the wreaths. Gardening scissors in hand, we all went in small groups to request our grandmother's neighbours if we could have some of their flowers. We targeted the neighbours we knew had the best gardens. Sometimes Yuva and her brothers would come and join us. I welcomed more hands because that meant more flowery loot. Many of the neighbours had gardens bursting with marigolds and lilies, sweet peas and roses, with fat bees flying drunkenly around them. In the evenings we followed our noses and walked in the direction of the houses where night-blooming jasmine, overcome by the dusk, suffused the air with its scent. The sweet smell wafted through the air and we took it all in, holding our breaths as if to imbue ourselves with the same sweetness.

Our neighbours always welcomed us. Our next-door neighbour Kong Swet, in particular, loved having us over. 'Ani! What are you children doing here? Come to pay us a visit?' Kong Swet asked.

'Em phi Aunty. We're here to collect flowers for the wreaths. It's Paieid's death anniversary next week,' I replied.

'Oh how nice, helping your Meieid. Come, come, pick the ones you want, and I'll give you a few,' she said as she ushered us into her garden.

Kong Swet helped us collect some of the flowers while her domestic worker offered all of us some orange juice.

'Te, this is enough em!' she eventually said as she hesitated near her thuja plant.

We knew when the neighbours asked us this that we had taken more than they were comfortable with. For the ones who were loath to cut some of their flowers, I would put my youngest cousin to the task as she was able to melt even the most parsimonious of them. They willingly gave us their marigolds and dahlias, the flowers they did not prize. We heaped our baskets with bright orange marigolds, puja flowers we called them, referring to their ubiquity during the Durga Puja season. I hated these flowers, their smell always made me feel sick. I would point at the roses, especially the white tree roses that smelled sweet. My grandmother had one of these trees in her garden. The flowers were always used in the special wreath shaped like a cross that I always carried.

'Give those seh Kong, they will look nice on the wreath,' I would say. But no one wanted to part with those, and the neighbours would decline, giving us the flimsiest of excuses.

Two evenings before 17 December, my grandmother called her friends over, and they all sat with cups of tea, making the wreaths. When I was younger I was not allowed to touch anything and could only hand them the things they needed as they dexterously weaved flower and fern onto the twig arch. It was a while before I was allowed to help my grandmother, and in time I was also allowed to call friends over to help. I only always called Yuva. My grandmother sat with her friends around the fire, with Yuva and I hovering by the sides as we pretended we were helping, handing them whatever they asked for, listening to them as they gossiped about the neighbours. Yuva never understood my grandmother and her friends completely so I would have to explain to her later in the evening or over the phone. Sometimes when they wanted to divulge the really scandalous gossip, they sent Yuva and me away in a sly manner, putting us to work making tea for them.

'Go make us a cup of sha,' Kong Philo said as she tied a flower to the wreath, clearly trying to get rid of us.

'Hooid go! Why are you just sitting here?' My grandmother admonished me.

'Toh toh,' I muttered grudgingly pulling on Yuva's arm as I screamed out, 'Bi! Theh sha!'

Once we all had our teacups in our hands, we sat on small round muras around the fireplace. When the embers stopped smouldering, the women edged closer to the fireplace and my grandmother shovelled coal into it, stoking the fire. The flames would choke and sputter as the fireplace was filled, and the women edged further away as it grew hot, and they began to sweat. I never sat too close that year because my mother had bought me a very expensive pair of sneakers, the first ones I owned. I could not risk the cinder falling on them. Those handling the wreaths could not sit too close to the fire or the flowers would wilt. I watched them as they nimbly put flower after flower, nestling them in fern, making a pattern on the twig frames. The floor was always littered with the dark green ferns, while the flowers were laid out safely in buckets. The smell of the thuja plant permeated the air as though we had brought my grandmother's entire garden in.

On the day of Paieid's death anniversary, all of us got into our cars early in the morning. The wreaths that had been lying on the bathroom floor all night were stacked in the cars, and we made our way to Lawmali. The Lawmali graveyard was on a gradual slope. A small tributary of the Wah Umkhrah ran alongside the asphalt road opposite the graveyard. Above it there was a steep hill that descended sharply into the little stream. On this hill there perched precariously many small houses, like cormorants on a seaside cliff. It would take only one disastrous earthquake to have them all crumble and fall into the muddy grey waters below.

Once we reached the graveyard, we parked on the side of the road, above the stream. We all carried one wreath each. I reached for the largest one. 'Iai that big one, I should carry it,' I said sanctimoniously.

'Why?' my sister asked.

'Because I'm the eldest.' No one questioned this and I had bullied the others into believing it was my birthright.

We climbed up the steady slope on the narrow crude path that had been cleared of grass. It must have been paved once because there were remnants of cemented flooring through which the weeds had pushed. There were pine trees flanking the sides of the graveyard, and their frail trunks bent obsequiously to the wind. We kicked the pinecones that lay on the ground on our way up. On each side of the path stood the gravestones, sombre and quiet. Some were tall and ornate, while others were just a bit of raised cemented flooring to mark where the grave was. Some of the graves were marked by crosses of wood or stone, others by small inconspicuous monoliths with names crudely carved into the stone. They stuck out of the ground like small crags on a hill. Those who could afford it, enclosed their graves within a metal, spiked enclosure with a gate that was kept locked. The others stayed unencumbered by any metal casing.

'Here lies
Livingston Khashiing
March 1934–September 2001
Beloved son, husband and father'

I imagined the grave probably housed a man who died of old age after living a full life. There were fresh flowers around his grave, which meant people remembered him and loved him. I almost resented his grave for having flowers when there were others that had none.

'Here lies Baby Boy
August 1986–October 1986
Taken from us too early
May he rest in peace'

There were graves like these, which made you feel something. Graves of children left unnamed. So small that anyone could have disregarded that the plastered mounds beneath their feet were occupied. Many of these graves were very old, and the white paint that had been painted on the cement was chipped and grey from the wind and the sun and the rain. They were all alone with nothing but the plump worms that wriggled for company.

Fresh graves protruded from the soggy soil, where the earth was too wet, and the body laid to rest was starting to turn cold. These graves had kwai and tympew placed inside the coffins—the betel nut and leaf serving as appropriate refreshments to take with them on their journey to the afterlife. Some held their occupants' favourite personal items: a favourite piece of clothing, a preferred snack or a bottle of whisky. My grandmother had placed a bottle of brandy in my grandfather's grave, his favourite. A mat or shylliah, made of bamboo husks, was placed in the hole in the earth before the coffin was lowered in. Money was also placed on the body. Earlier, people would place gold jewellery inside the coffin along with their loved ones. This practice grew rare when people heard of instances of pilferage by grave robbers.

There were also graves that were not marked. They were not paved with cement, had no paint on them, no flowers; they lay there undistinguished, like they were a part of the earth. There were no monoliths or crosses on these, no metal gates or wreaths. In them lay forgotten people from a forgotten time. People could have stepped on these graves not knowing that they were disturbing the remains of someone who could have been loved. Only those who paid attention could see that there was a raised mound of earth serving as the only marker that someone lay there. I pitied these graves, and sometimes uprooted dandelions that tittered under the winter sun to adorn them.

On reaching Paieid's grave, we opened the gates and placed our wreaths one by one. My grandmother had seen to it that the grave was cleaned, and a fresh coat of paint was given to the metal fencing a week before. Every year it was a new shade of red. She liked red. We then proceeded to place the candles on the grave. We lit them and were soon fidgeting as we waited for the prayers to begin.

'Keep quiet. Mei has to duwai now,' one of my aunts hissed poking her son on the shoulder as Mei bowed her head to pray.

'Khabrip ki khmat,' my grandmother whispered, asking us to close our eyes. She prayed in Khasi and then in English.

It was a solemn five minutes as we listened to her, trying to keep our eyes closed. When she was done, my grandmother wiped away the few tears that had rolled down her cheek. My mother, whose father's body we were praying over, looked at all of us, tight-lipped and calm. My aunts and uncle never said a word until we all proceeded to leave.

I tried to think of how my grandfather might have been. In their household, he was the patriarch. His was always the final word. In this matrilineal society, where the youngest daughter inherits the property, and the children take their mother's surname, the man is the head of the household. It is the kni or the maternal uncle who runs things. But in our house, it was Paieid. My mother spoke of him affectionately, describing him as a benevolent dictator. She told me he was intelligent and kind, but stubborn; that he never listened to anyone. She claimed that it shaped who she was, her voice heavy with respect.

The story my mother liked to recall about her father was about the time he brought shampoo to their home for the first time. My mother remembered him coming home and announcing to all of them, 'Step aside, woman! Do you know what this is? This is *shampoo*. It's special soap for the hair.' He had just come back from the market.

'Oh, how do you use it?' my grandmother asked, curious, looking at the small purple bottle he had placed on the kitchen table.

'You don't even know. I will tell you. Come here, one by one,' he scoffed, gratified that he had been asked and pointing to his children. 'Go wet your hair and come back here.'

They did as they were told and came back excitedly to the kitchen where he sat on the kitchen table. They lined up and submitted to the ministrations of their father. He lathered the soap on their hair and left it there.

'Now you wait and see,' he said. And so they waited and watched. For hours nothing happened. They stood there, shampoo dripping from their hair until the suds and lather hardened on their head and face. In the end my grandmother had to cut everyone's hair because the tangle were too painful when she tried to wash off the shampoo. My grandfather, looking sheepish, admitted to having made a mistake, and they all laughed about it later.

My grandmother spoke of him in admiring terms. 'He was very smart, pha. He had read all the encyclopaedias that you see in the drawing room. He read everything from magazines to big ponderous tomes.'

'We were not allowed to misbehave. He was very strict with us. Your father is a softy compared to him,' my mother told me. My grandmother, who enjoyed a certain amount of freedom living on her own as she did now, would not have been able to do so under the watch of my grandfather. 'Mei always had her head covered and dressed modestly around him. She never wore lipstick and always had her hair in a bun. She never spoke loudly or even spoke up at all,' my mother whispered as she spoke about my grandmother.

Years after he died, my grandmother cut her hair short and had it permed and dyed. She started wearing sparkly jaiñsems with matching shoes and earrings. She started living a life dictated by her own terms. Perhaps my grandfather would have grown to become malleable and changed with the times. I will never know. All I know is that he was an impressive man who had a tyrannical bent, and everyone respected or feared him.

My earliest memories of our trips to the graveyard were that of it being a very solemn occasion. No one spoke as we walked up the path, and no one spoke when we came back down after prayers. Mei would be much sadder then. I never knew how I was to behave. I was not sad because I had never known my grandfather, although I would have liked to. But as the years passed this solemnity gave way to a more relaxed feeling. We began to see it as a family excursion, a time we could stand huddled together over a grave on a cold morning with the sharp winter sun hitting our backs, our lips cracking, faces dry, our hands numb from the wind. And maybe that was the point of this annual exercise. It allowed us to remember those who have passed on, not in a reverential way with stiff sombre faces bowed over a cold stone structure, but in a mellow mood where we retold funny anecdotes. We became comfortable with the dead and more comfortable with our own dying.

In the later years, as we walked back down we made

lunch plans. We would go look at the other graves comparing who had the better flowers. My aunts felt comfortable enough to make jokes without receiving stern glances from their mother. We held each other's hands as we walked back to the cars to stop ourselves from slipping, as Nahduh told us stories.

Once, when she saw my cousin Fiona pick up a stick, my aunt whispered, 'You girls are playing with stuff you've picked from the graveyard! Haven't you heard that story about what happened to Rishi?'

We all shook our head. Nahduh walked toward Fiona and gestured to her to throw the stick down.

'Where did you get that?' she asked.

'I got it there, above that grave,' Fiona replied, pointing to a small unmarked grave which must have housed a child, judging from its size. 'It's a nice, smooth stick and I like it,' she said, startled by my aunt's reaction.

'Put it back! Don't touch or take anything from a graveyard. Don't you know it's bad luck?'

'Are you joking?' I asked, looking incredulous.

'I am not joking keiñ,' she said. 'You're not even supposed to enter your home with the shoes you have on now. You're basically carrying the dirt from the graveyard with you.'

'Nahduh, you please tell us the truth. I hate it when you start making stuff up.'

'I'm telling you. Look at what happened to Rishi,' she said dropping her voice almost to a whisper.

'Rishi? Your old driver?' I asked.

'Yes! That guy. You don't know what happened to him?'

'What happened?' I asked.

'He came to the graveyard with us once to drop off some flowers. When he was walking down he saw a white coloured stick, at least it looked like a stick. He unthinkingly broke it in two just for the heck of it.'

'Then what happened?' Fiona whispered as she leaned in closer to hear the story.

'He went home and lived happily ever after,' I said mockingly.

'You laugh now but you have not seen what I have seen.'

'Oh really? What is that?' By this time all the cousins were listening to her.

'It turns out that the stick he broke in half was actually a bone he had picked up from someone's grave. It was of an old woman's, and he had taken home the broken pieces with him. The old lady went to his house to get the pieces back. She went to his house and possessed him.'

'What? Please, that did not happen!' I dismissed.

Ignoring me, Nahduh continued, 'No one knew he was possessed at first. Then he got very sick. He had a high fever and became pale like a ghost. He did not sleep at night. He would toss and turn and call out to his mother. He would scream randomly. And on the third day, the lady who possessed him spoke out. She screamed, using his mouth for her voice. She claimed that he had hurt her when he broke that bone, and that he will have to suffer for disturbing her.'

'Oh come on! You know you're just making stuff up.'

'Ask Paduh,' she said, referring to my uncle. 'He saw this as well.'

'Then what happened?' Fiona asked after having gingerly placed the stick back where she found it.

'Oh then what, his whole family came and his mother brought out the broom. She beat him on the head with it till the spirit ran out of his body. You know our custom, dustur Khasi, is to use the broom to drive out spirits, em. Anyway,

Rishi has stopped going to graveyards now. He was pretty messed up after this.'

Nahduh maintained a straight face as she said all this. I did not know whether to believe her or not.

'Well we should not pick up things from the grave anyway. It's not respectful to the dead,' I said eventually with an air of finality.

'Yes, because you might end up like Rishi,' my aunt insisted gravely.

We all kept quiet while we ruminated on the story she had just told us. I had met Rishi. He seemed fine to me. He never struck me as the kind of person who would go and get himself possessed.

My aunt saw that she had done enough damage to her nieces and nephews and suggested we go to a nice restaurant for food. She even offered to take us to the ice cream parlour later. This was great news, and we all ran into the cars and made our way to the restaurant. We were told no more stories like Rishi's but even so in the subsequent years, no one dared pick up anything, not even me.

—

Years later, my friends and I were coming back from a college picnic late one evening. It was a long drive back from Daiñthlen, and my friend Lucy had an urgent need to use the facilities. We were crossing Lawmali graveyard when someone suggested that she run up and pee in the graveyard.

'I'm not peeing on a grave! I'm not a monster!' she exclaimed, shocked at the very irreverence of the idea. I agreed with her. 'Besides what if we anger some spirits and such,' Lucy said with the utmost seriousness.

'We will have to deal with more drunkards than ghosts,' I replied. She held my hand as we went and looked for a clearing where there were no graves.

The Lawmali graveyard never had a walled perimeter. One side of it led into a small wooded area, making it easier for trespassers to come through and disturb those resting. I had heard that teenage boys were beginning to use the graveyard as a place where they could drink. Many thieves had begun to steal the metal fences that guarded the graves. I thought of them stepping on the unmarked graves and it made me angry.

It was only four in the evening, but darkness had begun to set in. It always felt colder in the evenings when the sun had shone too strong during the day. The feather pink clouds spread across the sky as if they had come under my mother's rolling pin. The darkness began to overcome the orange skies. We looked up and saw Venus, and Lucy remarked, 'It's getting dark, my mom will kill me. Let's go.' She was done and ready to leave the graveyard, her eyes darting as if expecting a spirit to pass by.

At twilight the graveyard looked eerie and strange. As we were moving toward the car I saw nebulous shapes moving past the graves. When they came close enough I saw that it was a procession of people leaving the graveyard. No one said anything, and we could only hear the quiet sobs of the grieving people. The wind whistled, and the pine trees shook. All of us pulled our clothes tighter, hugging ourselves.

The men who had dug the grave seemed unperturbed by the cold as they walked with their trousers and their shirt sleeves rolled up. Their feet were caked in mud. The red earth was starting to dry and flake off their feet and hands, and they rubbed their hands hard so that the mud curled up in their palms and fell off onto the ground. The men made sure to stay at the back of the crowd and never joined the procession. Resting against the only wall of the graveyard, they lit a bidi and passed it between themselves.

Bishar Mary

Bishar Mary, who we would soon call just Bi, came to the house when I had just turned thirteen. I never knew her last name. I remember going to my grandmother's house one evening after school and seeing her in the kitchen by the sink as she washed rice. 'Kong, kumno?' I asked her politely.

'Kumne,' she greeted, smiling cheerfully, her voice mellifluous and her eyes twinkling. I called her Kong because it was the polite term used for any woman whose name you did not know or felt too awkward to use. That's what we called a maid, or a shopkeeper, or the lady you sat next to in church as you asked her to share with you the one hymn book in the pew. But when I moved closer, I saw that I knew her.

'Oh phi lah wan?' I asked surprised.

'Hooid,' she replied.

This was Bi who I had first met in Mairang, my grandfather's village. She was to be my grandmother's new maid. I never referred to her as that when talking about her. I always said 'helper' or 'nongiarap'. One time when referring to a maid I said 'nong trei', meaning a person who works. My mother corrected me, told me the term had a pejorative tone, and I only used the word 'helper' from then on.

Bi stayed in that house for the next decade and longer, until the time that I got married, taking care of my grandmother and everyone else who set foot in the house. When she first arrived she was not more than twenty-six. She was small and lithe, and her light skin was covered in freckles around her cheeks. We called freckles 'eit thyllah' which means flea droppings, and when I saw her face the phrase made sense. Bi had very long frizzy hair that she always kept in a bun. Her hair was thin, and the bun was barely the size of a baby's fist.

At twenty four, Bi had already had two children, both daughters. Her husband, if that was what you could call him, had left her alone to take care of their girls, her aging mother and herself. When she moved to work at my grandmother's house in Shillong, her daughters Diane and Bari stayed back in Mairang with her mother. They went to school there and would come to visit during the holidays. They grew up without their mother raising them, while she was in the city raising us.

Bi and her husband were not 'married' in the modern sense, although he was the father of her children. A lot of people in the villages, and many in the city, never performed any ceremonies to formalize a relationship between a man and a woman. There was never a need. When I was younger I always wondered about Kong Kyntiew, who stayed down the road from Mei's house. She had a baby before she was married.

'Why were you not invited for the wedding?' I asked Mei soon after Kong Kyntiew and her boyfriend had moved in together.

'Oh they shu iashong,' Mei replied.

'But they had a baby without getting married?' I asked perplexed.

'It's fine. They don't want to.'

It took me a while to understand this. Literally translated, 'iashong' means 'to live together'. Couples formed a union on the basis of their regard for each other and had children if and when they pleased. This was commonplace, and sometimes fuel for gossip. As I grew older, more people and even non-Christian Khasis, who earlier followed the informal iashong practice, began to conduct legal marriage ceremonies because with modern government came the need for paperwork and certification of these matters. Whether couples iashong or adopted legal methods, one was merely tolerated while the other was socially accepted. My friends and I used the term 'Khasi style' whenever a girl had a baby out of wedlock. A few of my classmates ended up getting a husband in the Khasi style.

I had been to Mairang, Bi and my grandfather's village, once when I was eleven. We had gone to visit my great grandmother. She lived there with other relatives, and Bi would often go over to help with the household work. My great grandmother's house stood in the middle of a large ground. It was a small wooden house that was painted pink only on one side. Sweet peas and snapdragons leaned against the wooden wall on the front, by the two stairs that led to the entrance. Bees buzzed around the flowers and we shouted 'buzzzzz' and waved at them to ward them off.

The car was never able to go up the steep dirt road to my

great grandmother's house, and we always had to get out and walk the rest of the way. A hillock stood at the far end of the grounds, and we climbed over it to see the wah. In the summer months the water rose high, bubbling loudly against the big rocks where women laid out their clothes to dry on huge rocks. They placed them flat against the boulders as they washed the remaining dirty clothes. Blue paste from the Rin bars stuck to the rocks. Squatting by the side of the stream in their aprons, their chequered jaiñ kyrshahs tucked under the thighs and knees, hair in a bun, and necks burning under the piercing sun, they kneaded the clothes. The clothes squelched under their knuckles like squealing piglets. Bi washed the clothes in the same way at my grandmother's home. The women gossiped and laughed as they rinsed their laundry in the cold river water. I felt that this was also a social gathering for many of these women who found ways to make the chore more enjoyable. It was a time away from the men and children, and tending to the house. It was a time to soak in the sun and sit near a stream while they talked about all the they left behind at home.

During our visit, my sister and I took off our shoes and tried to cross the stream. 'Peit bha!' the women warned us to watch our step when they saw us walk toward the water. We avoided the soapy rocks and tip-toed over the water. Sometimes we would step on a slimy stone green with moss and slip. The moss looked like wilted spinach that was stuck to the rocks and was difficult to avoid. My aunts were always there to make sure we did not hurt ourselves.

At my great grandmother's, we sat near the crude, stone stove on one side of the kitchen. Here she hung pieces of meat that had been dried and smoked. Bi helped her cut them into pieces and fry them. The fat sizzled in the pan, and the air was filled with the smell of charred pork and smoke. We ate this with rice and some boiled vegetables, biting our tongues as we chewed. We spent the night there, and by seven in the evening we went to bed. There were no televisions sets, and I could not read by candlelight. There were no bulbs there, no street lights, only the silvery moon and the sky perforated by the glistening stars.

'Do you have a TV sha Shillong?' Bi asked me once.

'Yes. We have one. Mei is planning to buy two,' I told her.

'Phi tip I sleep at five in the evening sometimes because it gets so boring here without a TV.'

'Ni! So early?'

'Te! There's nothing to do!' She whined and I nodded understandingly.

Bi moved to the city a couple of years after our first meeting and never had to worry about sleeping at five in the evening anymore. After my grandfather passed, my grandmother moved to a two-storey house in Lachumiere. It was too big a house for a small old lady to be living in alone. The ground floor was rented out as an office and Mei lived upstairs. The house had several guest rooms and three living rooms. There was a large garden outside with two ornate swings. The kitchen led out to a balcony that overlooked the office parking area below. Bi and Deng, the other helper, and whoever would later replace Deng, stayed with her in that large house.

During the holidays, in the winter months, my cousins and I stayed with our grandmother to give her company and pynsyaid ka iing, our presence needed to warm the house. On cold mornings we went out onto the balcony to sun ourselves. We giggled as we watched the helpers flirt with the office guards below. During orange season we cut oranges in a large bowl and made fruit salad. We used our hands to eat the spicy fruit salad as we sat with our backs turned toward the sun, taking turns and passing the bowl around to Bi, Deng and our grandmother.

Bi handled the cooking and the cleaning. We were not that close to Deng, and she left the house after staying only a year. Workers, or helpers, came and went, but Bi always stayed on. She listened to my grandmother complaining about how her flowers were wilting, or that the rice was not soft enough for her to chew. Every night she watched films with Mei and kept her company, making sure she switched off the lights the minute she heard Mei's soft snores. My grandmother, although she would not admit it, was very fond of Bi. 'She's a good worker. Very neat. But too slow,' was how she complimented her, high praise from a critical woman like my grandmother.

Indeed Bi was slow. She took her time to clean the dishes or scrub the floors. My grandmother would come bustling into the kitchen to help Bi everytime she had guests. 'Lah iap sliang,' my grandmother admonished, telling us that the guests were dying of thirst as she impatiently took the kettle away from Bi.

Bi always went along with everything my cousins and I did and never said no to any of my requests. Sometimes if I got very hungry I would convince her to help me make a snack.

'Toh seh Bi, I'm so hungry te,' I pleaded during these somnolent afternoons when everyone else was napping.

'Ni, you kids em, you just increase my workload,' she complained as she took out the pans. She turned on the stove, and we made candy by melting sugar in a pan and adding groundnuts. I had learnt the recipe in home science class. The amber caramel would harden in the pan and make it difficult for her to clean. Bi never told us she minded and would sit to eat the rock hard sweet candy with the rest of us.

During the weekends my cousins and I pretended we ran a beauty parlour and caked our faces and those of my cousins with a mixture of besan and honey, like how I saw my mother do it. 'Lah stick,' Bi squealed whenever I would put some on her face, and her face got sticky.

Mei did not like it if we played with the helpers or her driver too much. Whenever she felt irritated that they had not done something she wanted them to, she would scold them in front of us while scolding us in private for 'mingling too much' with the help.

'You can't be playing with them all the time. You should know your place. They are not here to entertain you,' my grandmother would lecture.

With regard to Dilip, her driver, Mei always told us that we should not touch his hands because he was a grown man, making me feel ashamed for something I could not quite understand when I was ten. It was different when I held Bi's hand and when I held Dilip's hand. I learnt that when my Mei scolded me. I never played 'Uma Joshi' and clapped my hands with Dilip again. For a while I was even hesitant to hold my cousin brother's hands because I thought then that young girls should not be holding any man's hands except her husband's.

This was the second time I remember feeling ashamed when I was a child. The first was when my mother took me to the big bazaar, Iewduh. There, after we had bought all the groceries we needed, I pestered her to buy me some cut pineapples. While she was paying for them and I was eating them, two men walked past me, and one of them pinched my cheek. It happened quickly and I was caught off guard. My mom saw this unfold and yelled after them. 'Hey!' She screamed, but the men ran away laughing. As we walked out of the bazaar, my mother pulled my arm as we walked, and scolded me. 'Why are you not more aware of your surroundings,' she hissed through her teeth. She pinched my hands as we walked fast and I knew not to answer back. I thought it was my fault those men pinched my cheek and I felt terribly ashamed, as if I had egged them on in some way. Years later when I remembered that incident I wondered whether my mother had been more angry with herself that day than with me, for having been unable to protect me. I didn't know if that interpretation was true because we never discussed it.

—

I first realized there was a greater barrier between the helpers and the rest of us when Bi's daughters first came to visit. They slept on mattresses laid on the floor in the living room near the fireplace, even though there was plenty of room in the guest rooms. After this, other small things became more evident, like how Bi would not eat on the same table as us but on a separate table. That both Bi and Deng did not have some of the luxuries that my family did. For the most part, when my Mei or any other adult wasn't paying attention, my cousins and I insisted that the helpers sit on the same table with us to eat, and I offered them wine in my granny's prized wine glasses on Christmas Eve, and sometimes even begged them to sleep in the same room as us after watching a particularly scary movie. We only put up the barriers when we were in front of my grandmother, who was a stickler for decorum.

Every Sunday evening we played 'poiñ'. This game was a version of seven stones, where one team had to stack up a pile of stones, and the other team had to stop them by using a ball to tag them out of the game. We shouted 'Poiñ!' whenever we hit someone. I think we made that rule up as we were playing. I made balls out of my grandmother's flesh-coloured stockings, feeding one to another until it was big enough to be pinched and knotted at the opening. The pairs riddled with lint and holes were always the first to be sacrificed for the game and we made sure Mei never caught us sneaking in her almirah. Bi helped me tie them into a strong knot. 'Kumne,' she showed and instructed us as she made one stocking cannibalize another.

The stones we used were lumpy, blanketed with bits of slimy moss that barely stayed in place. They slid off one another as soon as they were stacked, a real problem until one day Bi helped me find a solution.

'Let's take some of the slabs that are left over from the last renovation of the kitchen,' she said conspiratorially.

'I don't know where they are,' I replied, disappointed.

But Bi winked and took me to forage for these stones on the terrace. Here, there was leftover construction material and rubble and things from the renovations that took place at Mei's, some years ago. We found flat grey slabs that were used for flooring and knew these were the best ones for the job.

'Wow Bi, these are perfect!' I exclaimed, pinching her arm playfully.

'Adi! Pang!' She yelled out in pain, gratified that I appreciated her ingenuity.

We dusted off the mud and washed away the stains caused by the rusty tin cans of paint that the slabs had been in, and these became our permanent poiñ stones. We played with them until it got too dark to see and we had to swipe at moving figures and voices that shot out from the dark.

When we were done playing, Bi and the other helper made us all some tea. We sat in the kitchen, sweaty and tired, and discussed the game over pyllon shroiñ, the light, crunchy hard scones that we had with our tea. They floated on top of the tea like dinghies on still waters, till they soaked up enough liquid and sank to the bottom of the cup. I loved these crunchy treats. I always went with Bi to buy them from Mawkhar, near the big bazaar. Only one bakery in the entire city made these, a family that had been selling them for years from the ground floor of their generations-old Assam-type house. They also made bread and vanilla cake, but people went there mostly for the pyllon shroiñ. They raked them up in large, shovel-like scoopers and put them into brown paper bags while they were still hot. We held our packets close to our chests on cold days, warming ourselves as we ran out of the bakery.

On days when it rained and we could not play poiñ, Bi regaled us with stories of the people she knew who had fallen prey to the serpent Thleñ. I always coated any hair that fell off my head with saliva because she told me that was one way to keep off the Thleñ. The helpers sat and drank tea with us for only a little while till they had to start preparing the dinner, the signal being our grandmother's voice calling out, 'Da! Hep! Bah Bah!' A shrill intrusion, calling out to us to leave the helpers to their work, which signalled the end of playtime.

On Sunday evenings we took leisurely walks with Bi and, if my grandmother permitted, Deng would come along too.

We went down to Ward's Lake by the Governor's house, which was close to where Mei lived. The lake looked its best in November when the cherry blossoms were in bloom. Then the grounds were a pink haze we could see from a distance, the flowers on the trees bunched up like frothy pink clouds. We took the steep Lachumiere slope, tugging at the drooping branches from people's gardens as we walked by, down past the governmental offices and small bungalows. The garden area around the lake had benches with plenty of nooks and bushes for young couples to hide in. We got in line for tickets at the gate and bought roasted peanuts from the vendors outside while we waited. When we had enough money we bought pink cotton candy too, which was ten rupees more than we could usually afford.

Once inside we got on the wooden bridge, walked to the centre and fed the fattened fish. We threw peanuts at them, and in the murky green water their thick bodies pushed against each other as they reached out for these yellow pellets that floated at the top. As I looked at the fish from the bridge I would think sometimes of my grandfather's brother who committed suicide by jumping into this lake. I was told he was depressed, which is why he did it. Many people in the city, I had heard, had done the same. My mother never allowed us to get on the dinghy paddle boats because she was afraid, and because she was afraid, I also grew afraid and never sat on one. Instead, I contented myself by walking around the lake making fun of the couples who shielded themselves with umbrellas behind trees.

'Look at them!' my sister said each time, scandalized and pointing at the couples.

'Don't point! It's rude!' I shouted at her, as Bi and I giggled.

I was as curious as my younger sister to see what was going on behind the trees but I never showed it. She always pointed at the couples whenever we visited the lake. I was the elder one and I pretended to know what the couples were doing, imagining myself to be as well-versed with the ways of the world as Bi. In front of my younger sister I always fashioned myself as a sophisticated adult.

'Ni she is too much!' Bi muttered under her breath as she stifled a giggle and poked the other helper.

'Bi tell them what the couples are doing,' I said as we walked away from the couples, throwing a surreptitious glance when my curiosity got the better of me.

Bi and I liked to take walks to Laitumkhrah and Barik to eat puchkas. On some Sundays we walked all the way to the Golf Links where families laid out shylliahs and shawls on the dewy grass and had picnics. Children threw frisbees at each other, and couples walked from the first hole to the thirteenth, all the way up to Jungle Love, the forest where young couples went to be alone. We walked to Polo, up the road to Police Bazaar and ate hot jalebis dripping with syrup from Delhi Mistaan. But we could not go until I was done with my piano lessons. I hated going for lessons. 'Knowing how to play the piano will make you seem interesting,' my mother told me. I was less than convinced because I did not see the fun in it and thought it odd to bring it up in conversation just to seem interesting.

Bi and Deng dropped me to my lessons and waited for me to be finished. Sometimes during the week, when she was done with her evening chores, Mei would let Bi come and pick me up with the car from Mr Sarkar's house and we would stop by Kimba, the Chinese restaurant that used to be AVVA. On Sundays as there wasn't much work, both

Bi and Deng would come to pick me up after lessons. They sat together on the wooden bench outside the music room, sunning themselves while eating soh phi which they would buy from the vendors who walked around town with their khoh of seasonal fruits. They used this time away from my grandmother, who hated it when they gossiped, to talk about the neighbours and rake up stories from their villages.

The old lady who taught me the piano, Mrs Swer, reminded me of the severe nuns I would see at Loreto Convent. I waited for her on the cold wooden bench by the piano and practiced my scales until she came. She swooped into the room in her jaiñ kyrshah, which was always wet for some reason, and sat beside me, hitting my knuckles with her pen and saying, 'Wrong! Wrong! Lift your fingers!'

'I am, Miss!' I cried out as I blew on my knuckles to ease the pain.

Mrs Swer's white hair was always in a bun tied tight, as if to pull back not only her hair but also her aging skin. I loved her little cottage-like house with its roof clothed in pink and magenta bougainvillea. Hydrangeas and snapdragons lined the neat little soil beds under her windows. She had the prettiest rose garden I had seen, and we would barter seeds for rose stems. Bi waited as I convinced Mrs Swer to exchange a stem of her lilac roses for a stem of my mother's prized yellow ones. Whenever Bi could not pick me up, my mother would come. She loved to watch me bargain with the old lady as she bent down over her rose bushes, scissors in hand, slyly cutting off the most dried-up branch.

'Not that one, Miss, the one with the buds and flowers and where it is still green,' I said pointing it out to her as she narrowed her eyes and bent closer to the rose bushes.

'All right, all right,' she grumbled and grudgingly cut it off, handing it to me in a piece of paper. My mother would go home and laugh about this with my father.

--

I always wondered if Bi got lonely. When my cousins and I weren't around she only had Deng and my grandmother for company. She never spoke about her husband and my grandmother told me he was 'a good-for-nothing drunk'. I knew that she missed her daughters a great deal. They did not come to visit from Mairang too often. The journey was long and tiresome. They would have to catch a shared tourist taxi and endure the bumpy ride through broken, cracked roads. The roads were not well-made in Meghalaya, except the one outside the Governor's house that they kept topping off every six months or so. The materials used were always of the cheapest quality, and the rain always made them worse. Their family could also not afford to take trips frequently, so Bi rarely saw her children. Her mother would bring them over sometimes, and on those days Bi would be out all day. There was a time when my whole family went to Kolkata on a family vacation, and Bi called her two daughters and mother over to help her take care of the house and keep her company. I don't remember seeing her happier.

Bi was very pretty and attracted the attention of many interested suitors. This scared my grandmother because she was afraid that Bi would run off with someone or that she might get pregnant. My grandmother was always on the lookout, expecting Bi to succumb to someone's advances, and the other helpers spied willingly for her.

In time Mei's vigilance paid off, and she found out that Bi had formed an attachment with the guard who worked in the office below. By then she had been living for five years at my grandmother's place. Mei had intercepted letters that Bi and the guard were writing to each other. The guard's name was Ban. He was a stocky man who wore well-pressed shirts in different shades of brown. He barely spoke to us, but would always look up towards our balcony to wave hello.

'Kumno,' he greeted Bi every morning when she went out to throw soggy tea leaves in Mei's flowerpots.

'Kumne,' she replied, giggling. I rolled my eyes at both of them.

Ban slept in the afternoons in the shade, waking up whenever he thought he heard someone coming. He plucked pomegranates for us from the tree near the office that I was too scared to approach because of the patterned garden spiders that lounged on their webs in its branches. He always helped me remain hidden when I would go hide behind the steel almirahs in the office during games of hide and seek with my cousins. When Mei's kitten died, Ban helped us bury it in the garden under the large rhododendron trees next to the peripheral wall of the house.

Mei found out about the letters because the other helper had seen them exchanging notes and had quickly informed Mei of the same. Mei read the letters and was scandalized. The letters revealed that they would rendezvous when everyone was asleep, when the house's quiet was only punctuated by Mei's gentle snores.

'I don't even want to imagine what they do,' my grandmother exclaimed, as my aunt and I tried to suppress our laughter. We all sat huddled together near the iron rod heater in Mei's room as she asked us our opinion on the matter.

'Ni Mei! She is a grown woman. This was bound to happen,' my aunt said, smirking as she threw me a knowing look. I nodded as my aunt said this.

'What do you mean bound to happen?! This is my house! This is happening under my roof. This is an affront to my dignity,' she said angrily.

'But she has needs also na Mei,' Nahduh said. And at this point I could not restrain myself and we both burst out laughing.

'Phuit eh!' Mei cursed, spitting out the words. 'I was widowed when I was young and I never felt these needs you're talking about. These uneducated villagers should know better. Can she even afford to get pregnant again?!'

After she and I had wiped the tears of laughter from our eyes, my aunt asked in a serious tone, 'So what do you want to do now?'

'I'm going to talk to her and tell her if she's going to carry on like this I will have to let her go.'

'Mei, you be careful. You rely on her too much and she is an asset to this house. Think before you do something this drastic. You won't find anyone else like her. You need her.'

'I don't need anyone,' Mei said with an air of finality, and that was the end of that.

Nahduh looked at me when we walked out, remarking, 'A mother of four that *cannot imagine what they were doing* indeed,' throwing me a sly grin.

My Mei never shied away from a dirty joke, but she could become a prude when it suited her. When she found out I had a boyfriend, she decided to have a talk with me. 'A girl is like a delicate flower,' she told me. 'You have to wait for the right person to come and kheit you.' It was excruciatingly embarrassing, having the sex talk with my grandmother. And yet somehow our conversations did deter me from doing anything they did not like. I always found it hard to go against authoritative figures if they had given me a direct order. In addition to this, the fear of an unwanted pregnancy did loom over me. I did not want my grandmother's friends to be talking about me like they did about the local bureaucrat's daughter who had a son when she was fifteen. In my teenage years, dating a boy who was studying in a gospel seminary made abstinence not only easy but imperative.

The sex talk with my mother had been awkward too and consisted of a hurried conversation about venereal disease. I don't think Bi thought of venereal diseases. She was lonely and I was glad she was able to form an emotional and physical bond with someone after having been alone for so long. Mei did not see it that way.

Mei did eventually talk to Bi. I heard her from the other room as my sister and I tried to eavesdrop. We could not understand much as we sat crouched on her bathroom floor, trying to listen through her door. I only heard her distinctively say, 'Don't do this again,' as Bi got up to leave.

I think that after their conversation Bi was mostly embarrassed about being caught. My grandmother's fondness for Bi got the better of her puritanical leanings. So Bi stayed on, but after a week I saw that the office downstairs had a new guard.

I always wondered if Bi was sad to see Ban go. She never formed a romantic relation with any man after that. Sad to have disappointed my grandmother, she worked harder than she did before and seemed to us to forget about the guard. She rarely took holidays, and she even stayed back during Christmas that year because my grandmother could not handle the Christmas dinner herself. She only took days off for the Catholic Procession that would pass through the city. On those days she picked out her best jaiñsem, would put on earrings and lipstick, things she never put on in the house when she was working. Many old ladies did not like it if their helpers put on makeup, they considered them 'too fast', whatever that meant. But Bi went out on the days of the Procession, her lips painted and her hair in a smart bun, two pearl earrings dangling and her eyes shining, knowing she looked pretty. The Procession took place once every few months, Catholics dressed in their finest walking through the streets with crosses in their hands, heading toward churches to hear the message of God. We ran downstairs to buy icies from the ice cream men who, seeing a good business opportunity, sat by the side of the roads where the Procession passed. People came from all over, colourful shapes moving together like a wave, and we watched from the balcony, searching for Bi's familiar face in the crowd.

--

Instead of her two daughters, Bi watched us grow up: all thirteen of us, my cousins and I. She was there when I first got my period, and I was too embarrassed to tell anyone. She braved Bhaiti the shopkeeper to buy a packet of sanitary napkins for me. The shopkeeper liked to flirt and tease her.

'Kiska hai? Mei ka?' He asked slyly, guessing who they were for, pointing to the sanitary napkins she was asking for. He was hoping to elicit laughter with this crass joke about my aged grandmother.

'Ni Bhaiti! Don't ask too many questions!' Bi told him off.

When she had brought them home, she told me about

what Bhaiti had asked. I was glad I did not go buy the pads myself.

At thirteen I could show Bi my bloodied underwear and ask her to make sure if I had got my period. 'Peit seh Bi, dei ne em? I need pad ne em?' I knew I would not have been so open with anyone else. But as time passed and I grew older, I became less forthcoming with her. I was allowed to have friends over, or go out more, so my weekends were spent with friends instead. Bi would see me sneak into the house sometimes after being dropped off by my boyfriend.

'Mano that guy?' she teased, smiling because she already knew.

'No one phi,' I replied.

'No one keiñ!' she said disbelievingly.

Bi was as open with us as we were with her. If we were reticent, she never prodded further. She knew she could not pry about anything we did not go to her with first. She kept a safe distance from matters of the family, mindful that she was the help. There was that unspeakable barrier. As a child I did not see it, or perhaps thought I could breach it, so I took many liberties with her, much to Mei's displeasure. But by the time I was an adult, the divide between us was more visible to me, and it caused me to behave a little more formally with her. There was no more poiñ, and far fewer besan face masks. No more stories of Thleñ. We did not stop being close, but we did begin to treat each other like adults would.

When I was at university, Mei called me to tell me Bi was thinking of leaving. By then I was old enough to cook my own meals and had long overcome my embarrassment about buying sanitary pads. I had already started studying in Delhi and only saw Bi when I came home on vacation.

I could tell from Mei's voice that she was upset even though she pretended not to be. Time had passed. Bi had developed a few grey hairs; her kids had finished school; and her aged mother could not see as well as she could before. At about the same time Mei had taken a bad fall, causing her wrist to fracture and not be the same again. There were new neighbours next door who had cut down the orange trees that lined that side of the house, and the peach tree that grew in the backyard bore no more fruit. Mei's driver Dilip, who lived near the house, had died under mysterious circumstances. Mei felt bereft knowing that she would be without two people who had long been constants in her life, with Dilip's death and now Bi's impending departure.

Mei and Bi were still in discussions when I visited home a few weeks later. Mei tried to convince her to stay but she could not.

'Shong se Bi. I'll raise your salary,' I heard my grandmother say. I was eager to listen to what was happening. I pretended I needed a nail cutter, busying myself over the dressing table in Mei's room as they spoke near the bed.

'Em phi, my Mei is growing old, and she needs someone to care for her. Trust me I would stay back if I could,' Bi said.

'Toh, if you have decided then I won't force you,' Mei sighed loudly, disappointment apparent on her papery face. She knew there was merit in Bi's reason to leave.

On her last day at Mei's house, Bi and I made sticky groundnut caramel one last time. She told me she would miss us all and asked us to visit her in Mairang. I didn't know if or when that would happen. We spoke of our days playing poiñ and I asked after her children. One was in college now. I told her about Delhi and how alien it was to Shillong. She told me she would never want to go there. I asked her if she would miss us, even though I knew she would, because I wanted to hear her say it out loud.

'Haoid kein ngan miss!' She affirmed, surprised that I could ask her such a question.

'Shwa ban mih, you want to have some tea with me?' I asked her as she was about to leave. She nodded and we sat together at the dinner table, pouring out whatever tea was left in the kettle. We pulled out a spoon each from the rack and dunked a pyllon shroiñ in our teacups. Mei came in to see what we were doing in the kitchen. She made small talk, loneliness setting in, and we listened to her patiently as the pyllon shroiñ slowly sank into the warm tea.

The Revival

God would remain the same amorphous, baseless entity I worshipped at twenty as he had been when I was introduced to him at eight. It was the age at which I first went to church, where prayers escaped our mouths, floated up vaulted ceilings and slipped through the cracks in the walls to reach God like a balloon I had let slip through my fingers.

Sunday school was my first foray into the house of God. Just as a baby is weaned or sent to kindergarten, Sunday school was how I was initiated into religion. I enjoyed Sunday school. I sat in our tiny classroom, enthralled, as we were taught stories from the Bible. All the children were taught in different classrooms depending on their age. The classrooms were situated in the few vacant rooms at the back of the church. The older children had their classes outside on plastic chairs that wobbled and wilted in the sun. The room we sat in was dark and bare. The chairs were always coated with dust, a light brown coating that settled like a shroud, gathered through the week when the room remained empty. We used the handkerchiefs our mothers pinned to the front of our dresses to wipe it away. Sometimes we drew on the dust with our fingers, outlining faces and houses even though none of us were allowed to get dirt on our Sunday best. There was a small blackboard on one side of the wall which the rain had damaged, its surface bulgy and the wood beneath exposed. They still used it. When I had just joined we were taught parables and about Noah, Moses and Jonah. We sang songs during our lessons: 'Zacharias was a very little man and a very little man was he...'

There was a Miss Judy who taught me when I was eleven, and I liked her very much. She had short hair, freckles on her face, wore frosty pink lipstick and always had a guitar. She was young and unmarried and taught us songs. I was always in the church choir and loved going for practice in the evenings on Saturdays. It served as an excuse to get out of the house and meet my Sunday school friends. My mother had hoped I would play the organ in the church, but I never stuck to my piano lessons with Mrs Swer long enough to play well. Choir practice usually lasted an hour and a half. We all stood by the pulpit, under the curved, high ceilings, the evening sun shining through the coloured windows reflecting diamond shapes on the floor and pews like we were looking through a kaleidoscope. We stood next to the large dusty organ which vibrated and expelled music one note at a time like whales in the ocean spouting out their song. It clicked every time the organist first pressed on the keys, after which it moaned under the weight of his finger. Our voices reverberated in the hall as we sang in harmonies. The man on the organ, the music teacher, his face leathery and sweating, would stop us intermittently and ask us to go along with the tune. 'I can't hear you sopranos, some of you sound flat!'

Miss Judy smiled and played her guitar in tune with him. This practice was in preparation for the World Sunday School Day which was held every year in November. On this day the children of the Sunday school were given prizes for doing well in the Bible study exam held a month prior to it. Parents came to see their children perform and win prizes. I stood at the front of the church with the rest of the choir, shivering with excitement in my new dress, waiting for us to begin the song we had been practicing all the days leading up to this event. Cameras flashed in front of us, blinding us temporarily, and I tried to avoid eye contact with the crowd. One year I won first prize. I was given a hardbound book on the story of Noah and his ark. The cover was sky blue and glossy, and it made me giddy with glee. It now rests in a cabinet in my home in pristine condition, standing proud next to my father's prized hardbound finds.

We had a teacher who liked to rush through lessons so he could quiz us on topics of general knowledge. We called him Bah Dan. He and many of the girls found quizzing more enjoyable than regular Sunday school lessons.

'You want to continue the lesson?' he asked all of us in the class.

'No, sir!' we shouted each time he asked.

'Should I leave and let you people off?' he teased us further.

To which we replied with, 'Quiz, Sir! Quiz!'

He was a stocky man who wore spectacles so small that they barely covered his eyes, looking like a pair of old-fashioned pince-nez. His hair was cut very short, and his face was always sweaty as if he was continuously working over a hot stove. He carried a stack of cards with him that had questions printed on them. This stack he placed safely in his front shirt pocket to make sure the girls saw he was carrying it. We all liked to answer the questions to impress him and each other, caring very little for the bookmarks that were handed out if we answered correctly. Some girls were able to answer so many questions that every second page of their Bibles had a bookmark. The colourful strings stuck out from between the pages like lizards' tails, and the girls showed them off proudly like spoils of war. Each had an inspirational quote, 'God will take care of you'. I only won two.

I was affiliated with the Presbyterian Church. My father is a Catholic and, out of curiosity, I had gone with him to the Catholic grotto one time. It was a large church painted a strange grey-blue that, on days when the fog was too thick, was still able to pierce through the gloom. It was quite the tourist attraction. As soon as you entered the church there was a fount where the holy water was kept. From the foyer you could see the light from the candles flicker. The wind would come hurtling into the church through the open doors and the flames would dance as if trying to elude it. These were candles lit by the people who would come and drop a donation in the square wooden box near the altar. On one side of the church above the altar stood the statue of Mary and her newborn child. She was dressed in blue and looked cherubic. The right side of the church had stained glass which had scenes from the Passion of Christ, and the other side had the saints in various poses. They looked mournfully at the devotees kneeling in the pews, the sun projecting colours through them and into the dimly-lit hall. I was awed by the grandeur of this church and the Catholic church's many ritualistic methods of praying. It intimidated me. I remember that at one point, during the prayers, one was to turn to the person next to them, mumble something and nod. I did not know what to do and was thoroughly embarrassed for it.

My mother is a Presbyterian, and my parents both preferred that I remained in that church too. When I turned sixteen they asked me, 'Would you like to continue going to the Presbyterian church? Or would you like to start at the Catholic church?'

'They're both the same to me. It's the same God. Makes no difference,' I replied, gratified that they asked, feeling like my opinion mattered.

'Ok toh. Stay in the same church then. It will just be less of a hassle,' they said, and I did.

The Presbyterian church at Police Bazaar which I attended had no statue of Mary, or high ceilings or large ornate windows. It was rather modest with its mid-sized windows, its large and simple wooden cross that hung on the side of the pulpit and the giant clock. The people would impatiently look to this clock when the preacher had gone on too long. The clock was first placed at the front, near the altar, but when those who ran the church saw that it served only as a distraction they put the clock at the back of the room instead. This way people would have to turn their heads to look at the time, and they knew the congregants would be too shy to do so. The clock stood in full view of the pastor who delivered the sermon. I remember during one sermon seeing a man using his index finger to tap his watch as if hoping he could bully time into going faster. The pastor brought attention to it.

'Te, I think I should end today's message now. I might

have gone on too long I'm afraid. The gentleman tapping his watch so vigorously has reminded me that I only have thirty minutes.' He said this good-humouredly and the congregation laughed out loud, waking up several who were drooling over their Bibles.

On regular days a purple velvet cloth was used to adorn the pulpit from where the pastor delivered his sermons. On special days like Easter or Christmas they brought out a white velvet cloth with its gold-embossed cross in the centre with golden trimmings. Just like the pulpit, the rest of the congregation dressed more ostentatiously. When I got older, I overheard complaints that people went to church just to show off, driving to church in their giant cars and walking through church halls in their expensive clothes. I suppose it was true for many.

The church was run by three siblings who took care of the day-to-day dealings. There were two brothers and a younger sister. The sister was very well-dressed and we all loved to look at what she wore to church each week. The three were very dedicated to the work of the church. The two brothers remained single through their lives; however their sister did eventually get married when she was much older.

'It was the Welsh that founded the Presbyterian church in Meghalaya more than a hundred years ago,' my father told me one evening when I asked him. 'Like other Christian missionaries, they trampled through the forest-covered hills of the North East to convert a sequestered population of tribespeople.'

'But why?' I asked him.

'Because they were doing the Lord's work,' he said with an air of finality.

Years later, when I went to visit a pastor in his home, I saw a wall hanging which had a poem in Welsh woven on it. It reminded me of how much of an impact a small group of Welshmen had had on an entire people.

At the Presbyterian church I went to, the lessons and service were in English. Yuva would often come with me to this church starting from when we were in the fifth standard. She enjoyed the pageantry and I loved having a friend to sit with and nudge when the sermons got too long. I also liked to show her the boys I had a crush on at the time. Sometimes I attended service in the large Khasi church in Mawkhar, of which my regular, smaller church was an extension. I only went to the Mawkhar one to accompany my grandmother. It was a large church right in the centre of the city down the road from Motphran. This made it easy to find because everyone knew Motphran, a brick structure erected by the British to commemorate the Khasi men who died serving the English in France during the First World War. My mother told me it was meant to be Mot France but the locals could not pronounce it, and it became known as Motphran. The Mawkhar church was painted a mint green with a silver gate that glinted in the sun. Plump dahlias leaned sleepily against the walls outside. It was intimidating inside, with a pulpit larger and further away from the congregants than what I had seen in other churches. The seats were low and hard against my bottom. I complained about it once. 'Mom, the seats are too hard and it hurts.'

'Think about Jesus's hardships when you make petty complaints like this,' she chided.

When I was younger and my feet would not reach the floor, I could not see the preacher from where I sat. At least not all of him. I saw only his head and heard his voice as it echoed in the hall. Every time the pastor said, 'Toh ngin ya duwai,' asking us to bow our heads to pray, I started to fidget so much that my grandmother had to throw stern glances at me. The pastors preached in Khasi that was too flowery for me to understand. Their voices shook and trembled while they delivered their sermon. I paid attention to each glottal stop and trill, and it sounded to me as if they were gargling water. There was such an urgency in their voice that it felt that one could expect the rapture that very evening over tea. Most people would sleep through this din, waking up only to swat flies that came and rested on their sticky faces. When I broke up with one of my boyfriends I would come to the Khasi church diligently, hoping I would catch a glimpse of my ex. I always did, and the benediction at the end of the service was always recited by me bleary-eyed and choking down tears.

By the time I had started going to church, eighty percent of the population in Shillong was Christian. Tourists coming to Meghalaya would complain that everything was shut on Sunday. My grandmother converted to Christianity when she was just sixteen years old. She did it before anyone else in her family. 'My late grandfather, your great great grandfather, was one of the Lyngdohs of Mawphlang. That meant he was a priest, and he performed rituals as per the customs of the Niam Tynrai, the monotheistic religion of the Khasis. He used to perfom sacrifices, kniah, by cutting up a chicken or goat. He did this in order to help people dispel curses, and overcome fear of the evil eye', my grandmother told me.

'Like a shaman?' I asked curiously.

'I do not know what that is, but he was an important personage in society. But this did not deter him from converting to Christianity later, nor did he stop me, his granddaughter, from converting. He converted long after I did, when he felt the time had come, risking a fall in station.'

'Wow, why?'

'Because he felt the Lord call to him I suppose,' she said.

My grandmother, although a converted Christian, was not hesitant to go to the Lyngdoh when she was worried about her son. As a baby, my uncle had not begun to walk even when he was three, much to the consternation of his mother. She felt perhaps there were some other forces at play and went to a Lyngdoh. He performed the egg breaking ritual.

As my aunt related to me, 'They found a hair inside the egg. It was a sign of some curse or evil eye voodoo thing that people had placed on your uncle. I don't know how far it is true. Anyway the Lyngdoh took it out and he could walk after that day.'

As I got older I continued to go to church, finding some solace in it. I liked the calm that prayer offered, and it provided a form of anchorage in my adolescent life. I went to church when I did badly in school or if I sensed my parents were having financial trouble. I lit candles in the Catholic grotto when I broke my mother's favourite Borosil tray. I went to church diligently especially when I wanted to get out of the house when my mother was being difficult, and I needed a few hours away from her.

When I was nineteen, I became infatuated with a boy, Daniel, who was studying to be a pastor. We met when we were studying in the same college. He left after studying History for a year so he could study Theology in Kerala, but we continued to date long distance. I had never had a boyfriend before this. Some of the girls in my school thought it was inexplicable that someone like me would have a boyfriend. I found this joke to be particularly hurtful.

For Daniel, dating consisted of short, ten-minute phone calls on his seminary's landline, hoping none of the seminary's padres were listening in on us from another line. I spoke to him on the landline because he was not allowed to keep a mobile phone. He was allowed only two calls a week: one he saved for me and one for his parents. I would wait in a PCO at four in the evening every Wednesday after college and dial the landline number. As I waited for it to connect, I read the handwritten scribbling on the wall, running my finger over 'Rajesh loves Mona'. The phone would ring four times before I heard a click and someone on the other side saying, 'Gospel for Asia Biblical Seminary, yes?' After being told to hold and an agonising wait, I would hear a second click, and then there was Daniel, saying, 'Hello.'

We dated for a while and in that time, my visits to church became more frequent. It was Daniel's determination and resolve that I respected, I realized. It was what made me stick around with him even when he was being difficult. Eventually, we fell apart. I was bitter at first, but I got over it faster than I thought I would. For years, I wondered if he was still full of the same zeal to work in the church that he had when I first met him. I suspected somewhere along the way he lost his way, like a sheep who wandered away from the flock.

--

At this time in Meghalaya, in the fall of 2006, strange happenings gripped the state. I was in my second year of college then. I don't remember how and when it all started, but schoolchildren had started succumbing to a kind of fit or seizure. As they stood in assembly halls in their school and while their principals addressed them on day-to-day matters, many seemed to be struck down by some invisible force and fell to the floor. They shook and convulsed on the floor like they were possessed, and those who watched remained helpless. They muttered out loud incomprehensibly, and when they recovered they claimed they had seen visions. Many wailed and wept and needed to be taken out of the hall. This happened in many schools and it frightened bystanders.

The church elders claimed that the Holy Spirit was descending into the children. They called it the 'Revival'. In a particularly impassioned sermon one evening, a pastor lectured us on why he believed this was happening to people. 'This is a sign from God,' he thundered, 'a sign that we need to look inward and reflect on our actions. We need to renew our ties with God.'

I remember my sister coming home one evening and telling me, 'Ei, you remember Cornelius? My classmate? He fell on the floor and had one of those fits today. He had the Revival everyone is talking about.'

'Where did this happen?' I asked, intrigued.

'It happened in class, during lessons. It was very boring and so hot. We were all starting to fall asleep, and then all of a sudden he started shaking. It was very scary. The teachers didn't know what to do. They tried to carry him, but they were scared to touch him while he was in that state. When he stopped shaking, they called for a stretcher and took him home.'

My mother, ever the sceptic, remarked, 'Who knows what is happening?'

The church saw a rise in membership and it could not be happier. Videos were circulating of a glowing wooden cross and an image of Christ next to it. People said this had happened in a church in Malki. Needless to say, people flocked to the church in droves to see this miracle. I never saw it and never bothered to go. I was sceptical, and I hated crowds. But as school after school fell to this celestial malady, people who were agnostic turned devout and even sceptics started to waiver in their disbelief. I never saw anything happen with my own eyes. The only accounts I heard were either from my sister or my two aunts who both taught in schools. The newspapers started to report on it and it was all anybody could talk about.

A year before the Revival began, I had attended a Bible camp. I had gone with many friends and although the lessons left me bored, it was fun to camp out in nature away from the prying eyes of my parents. It was on a large, private property that had a basketball court where we played our games. I loved the evenings best, when we would all have tea and sit outside for ten minutes before we went back to our lessons. We slept on bunk beds and the other girls told me their reasons for coming to the camp. They ranged from guilt for having had premarital sex, to drinking too much, or just wanting to spend time with friends. Every morning at five, our friend Gary rang the bell to wake us up for our early morning prayers. I always went to prayers sleepy because the night before had been spent talking till late.

Our days at camp consisted of lectures and team-building exercises. We had a fixed routine we followed every day. Lessons, singing, games and prayers. The lady who was in charge was a pious disciplinarian who would not let Daniel and I be alone for more than a minute.

'I don't want you to stray, Daniel,' she said one evening after she had interrupted us as we had tea together outside by the basketball court. She used every metaphor and simile she could for sex.

'You can trust us, aunty,' Daniel told her.

'I trust you,' she said as she threw me a dirty look, making me feel like quite the Jezebel. She was overbearing and controlling but spoke in such a saccharine way that it was hard to tell her off. She made a great show of her piety. It was on leaving Bible camp that I learnt that the gossip about town was that her husband was one of the most corrupt government officials around.

Two major lectures took place each day at camp, one before lunch and one before dinner. I was never a fan of these and the smell of food wafting through the kitchen never helped. The metal chairs we sat on were very uncomfortable, and they made dozing off impossible. On the second day, the lecture was about hell, and how we could get to heaven. The lecturer droned on and I was beginning to nod off when I heard him say that Gandhi was definitely going to hell. I woke up with a jerk, turned to my friend and mouthed, 'What?!'

I was wondering what I had missed. Someone else who was clearly disturbed by this raised his hand and asked, 'But Gandhi was in the freedom struggle, surely he will be in heaven?'

'Well he is not a born-again Christian so he definitely is not going to heaven.' The lecturers' voice was firm.

'But, sir, then that means all the people who did good things and are not Christians are going to hell. That can't be right,' I quipped. Many nodded. Daniel and a few others shook their heads in disagreement to what I had said. The room started to buzz as everyone started talking among themselves.

'See children, you are all getting very worked up,' the lecturer tried to make himself heard over our talking. But his statements had made quite a stir and we continued to speak about this through the evening. Daniel was adamant that the lecturer was right.

'You don't get it,' he said to Gary and me.

'So explain it to us because it all seems very extreme,' Gary said.

'Yeah, so it does not matter how good you are on earth because if you aren't a born-again Christian you are damned? That makes no sense!' I was almost shouting. Daniel refused to engage with us that night, and Gary and I were left to question everything we had been taught.

On the third day we were there, the lecture was not as polarizing as it had been the day before. It was a particularly warm evening, and all the windows had been left open so the cool breeze would be allowed in. Mosquitoes, following the light in the room, came and feasted on our blood as we slapped our knees and shins. Giant grey moths clung to the lights and lizards crawled into the room, watching from the ceiling as we tried to stay awake.

When the lecture was over, we were asked to bow down our heads in prayer. Looking at us, the preacher loudly said, 'If anyone among you wants to open your heart to the Holy Spirit, come forward. Now is the time.'

This was new to me, but not to others. People began to raise their hands and pray loudly with vehement urgency and energy. Their voices filled the air and I peeked through half-closed lids as I slapped away a giant mosquito that sat on my arm. Just as more people raised their hands, a girl started wailing and fell to the floor. She hit the ground with a dull thud, like a stone falling flat on the water, barely missing the metal chairs. The people next to her moved aside and gave way. Eyes open, I was just about to yell out for help when I heard a voice say, calmly:

'Anyone else overcome by the spirit, feel free to let go.'

I turned toward the voice. It was the preacher.

'Succumb to the word, and if anyone wants to give their hearts to God, speak now. Accept him as your holy saviour,' he said, his face donning a pained expression, his hands in the air, his body swaying. Someone on the side strummed the guitar softly, and more people stood up from their seats. Everyone else still had their eyes shut. I only then realized that this was part of the prayer and that no one was having an epileptic fit.

Again, the preacher said, 'If we are truly one with God and are true Christians, we will accept him as our one and only God.'

I sat there, utterly confused. 'Have we not already accepted him as our one and only God? We all are Christians here,' I thought to myself.

As these thoughts ran through my head, I peered at Daniel, who still sat next to me. He had not stood up like the others. I heaved a sigh of relief. 'This is fine,' I reasoned, as I surreptitiously turned to see how many people had raised their hands and how many of us were damned. In that cold, small room, all I could see and hear was the screech of metal chairs as people stood up to raise their hands and cry. Every time a metal chair scraped against the marble floor, I winced.

When class was over, we all went for dinner and everyone acted like nothing had happened. I wanted answers. I asked the people who, like me, had remained seated. They shrugged and one of them explained, 'This is what happens. You don't have to worry. Do not stand up unless you want to.'

'But what does this all mean,' I asked. No one could give me a satisfactory reply.

The next day, as I walked into that classroom, I prayed that the metal chairs remained stationary and that yesterday's frenzied, impassioned episodes of worship were not repeated. I gazed around the room. The walls were blue and the sun that shone through the window from the east cast our shadows on the wall. Eventually the wailing and the fainting began, and I turned to look at the shadows as I dared not look at the people. Shadow after shadow answered the call. They fell to the floor like dominos. The hairs on the back of my neck stood on end; I felt a chill and then I started to sweat.

When I peeked at Daniel, I saw that he had stood up too. Today I was alone in my doubt, and I felt limited. I did not want to stand for something I was confused about, nor did I want to stand because the others were doing it. But I was frightened of being outed as a person who was not repentant or godly enough. I stayed put on my chair as if an invisible force was weighing me down. The metal seat felt cold yet familiar against my thighs. I was one of three people who had not stood up.

Throughout the duration of the camp other kids tried to explain to me what that whole exercise meant. They told me what being a 'born-again Christian' was. I pretended to understand and left the camp more confused than when I had stepped in.

Like my mother, I too was sceptical of the Revival. But try as I did to find a logical explanation for it, I could not. Everyday someone would demolish any rational analysis I could come up with.

The religious nuts in my college were overjoyed. 'It's like they said in Revelations,' I overheard one of them say to the other as I crossed them on my way to class. They were certain it would soon be time for the rapture. They condemned all the other college students who showed no interest in the Revival. Once, I had gone out to have a drink with some friends who many of these extremely religious kids had condemned as 'ungodly'. They caught up to me the next day before class and began to lecture me. 'As the girlfriend of a future pastor you should not be flirting with the devil by sitting with them,' they chided.

'Flirting with the devil?! That's a bit much,' I said, trying to control my laughter. 'Whatever happened to "love thy neighbour", and "he who is without sin cast the first stone"?'

'You better watch out mo, the end of days are coming.'

I thought this was all very amusing. I relayed everything to Yuva in the evening when we spoke on the phone. 'Yes, they are all acting very cult-like and scary. I just want them to stop proselytizing on the basketball court. It's making the rest of us uncomfortable.'

'At least something is going on back there. The Mumbai rains are making it hard for me to even get to college,' she complained from the other side. She had already started going to college in Mumbai by then and always wanted updates on what was happening at home.

During the time of the Revival, Sundays saw more people on the road. Women walked to church in their heels. They walked up and down slopes with their jaiñsems and mekhlas on, as their other hand held their Bibles, purses tucked under their arm. The men walked side by side, finishing their cigarettes before they entered the church. Cars lined the roads outside of churches, making finding a parking spot difficult for everyone. The beggars waited outside the church and did better in these times as people loosened their purse strings without hesitation.

Somehow, I saw very little change at my modest Presbyterian church, for which I was glad. By the time the Revival was accepted as a city-wide phenomenon that was not just isolated to two or three churches or schools, miracles and hoaxes began to occur in equal measure. Some were struck down by an invisible force that no one could explain, while others saw the merits of being seen as 'revived' and performed the pantomime. Children did this to get out of class, shouting gibberish, enjoying the confusion it created. It allowed them to escape tests and stay home from school. Machiavellian adults did this to get out of marriages, or get into them. One lady told a man she barely knew that in a vision she had had during her Revival episode, she had seen herself marrying him. The man, being a devout Christian, although loath to marry her, did so. He did not want to go against something that he believed was nothing short of a miracle and, in all possibility, a message from God. They got married. They were both unhappy after.

Some lied and said they had had the Revival so they could boast and get admiration. A girl in my college, who I knew had not even seen the inside of a church, was speaking to a crowd one morning, enthralled. A group of people had gathered around her as she told them of the visions she had seen.

'I remember feeling full. Like I had just had a big lunch. Then I saw only darkness,' Charlene whispered to her captivated audience, quite the raconteur. 'Then I woke up and saw two large golden doors.'

At that time, curious about the gathering, I had edged closer to listen to her.

'Then the doors opened. I saw only clouds and a blue sky,' she continued, 'and then I heard the voice of God.' Charlene paused for effect; 'God said in a loud, deep voice: "Ask me anything, my child, and I will tell you the truth."'

'What did you ask him?' the girls sitting next to her squealed impatiently,

'Since God told me I could ask him anything, I asked him if I should go out with that guy who asked me out yesterday.'

As she said this, I burst into laughter and was soon joined by many others. Charlene could no longer continue. The crowds started to disperse, shaking their heads. Only the girls sitting next to her bothered to ask her about the reply God gave to Charlene's question: 'And then what did he say?' we heard them ask her as we walked back to class.

Nobody from my family was touched by the Revival. Perhaps we were all too sceptical to be open to such a thing as this. Maybe the miracle passed us by like the sickness passed by the Hebrews in Egypt. Teatime after college was spent discussing who had been revived. My cousins and I made Maggi and sat by the fire while we discussed these matters. A distant cousin of ours had fallen to it. He was a spoilt teenager who had always been given everything he asked for, so when he was taken by the Revival, most of the family laughed because we thought it was some kind of joke. I told my cousins about the kids I knew in college who had been revived, who proclaimed, 'We're going to stop drinking and smoking now. We backslid all our lives, now we want to be better.' It was not long before they went back to doing what they were doing before the Revival had struck them with fear for their souls.

In time, the number of people seeing visions and fainting reduced. The first waves of the Revival began to recede and eventually it stopped altogether. My cousins and I ran out of stories from our colleges and schools. Fewer cars lined the roads, men smoked their cigarettes and walked past the church, and the beggars could not rely on the churchgoers' magnanimity on Sundays. By Christmas we would only hear about a few scattered incidents here and there. But at the end of that year, the carollers sang with greater zeal and the priests and pastors thanked God for the Revival.

The city went back to normal, and I waited for my small sleepy town to be gripped by another scandal or occurrence and for the local papers to report on other odd news. By the New Year, people became obsessed with the rumour that Michael Owen, the world-renowned football player from England, was actually from Mawkyrwat. He was not. It was a case of mistaken identity. However, people refused to believe he was not from Meghalaya, and they had rabid fights over this matter.

Things remained mostly unchanged for the town after the Revival. It had descended like a thick, heavy mist, and people groped about in this fog for their faith. People needing crosses to appear on walls showed that they too were struggling with questions about God, just like I was. I continued to go to church whenever I could, finding solace in the click of the organ and the clink of the offerings bag. I saw the same familiar faces and new ones who I reckoned had had their faith reinvigorated. The pastor still spoke about trusting God and warned us against sinning. The caretaker of the church, meanwhile, had run off with three crore of the church's savings. On rainy days there were fewer people in the church, and on days closer to the board exams they had to put in extra plastic chairs to accommodate the expanded numbers. I enjoyed watching the pastor struggle with the projector as he tried to project the lyrics to a hymn on the wall, and I waited patiently when the overzealous treasurer prayed for what felt like hours.

In these familiar surroundings I felt a calm that drew me closer to God. I knew this God, the God that enabled me to find solace in these things, the God that shone through the familiar coloured triangles onto the floor and filled me with joy as I belted out a hymn.

Yuva

At ten, I understood mortality. I learnt it that one summer evening when I caught and placed ten milky white butterflies in a large empty Horlicks glass jar on the insistence of Bah Rit, my friend and neighbour.

'Ale kein, we shall catch a few, it's fun,' he convinced me that evening.

'Where?' I asked.

'The football field kein biej,' he said, talking about the open field near the house where the butterflies perched on dandelions by the brambles and weeds.

We crossed the road from my house and began our hunt. After it got too dark to look for them I began to get bored. 'Kein noh,' I shouted at Bah Rit when I had had enough, and there was not enough space for the new ones he was catching. Like with all pretty things, we wanted to possess them. We placed them in a glass jar after we had poked holes in the lid so they could breathe. They felt frail and buttery against our fingers like the greased paper with which my mother would line cake tins before baking. I saw them try to escape, colliding against the glass until they sank to the bottom of the jar. Many of them lost their wings as they struggled and languished in this glass crypt. I grew worried when I saw them start to crumple down and, in an attempt to save them, I opened the lid and tipped it over. They all dropped in a white powdery heap on the ground. None of them had survived. In that moment, my inchoate mind understood that life is a thing that can be taken away. That I was complicit in the death of a living being, and that things can fade and die. That wings can fall off and sometimes things cannot be saved. Mortality is an ensnared butterfly dying in a glass jar.

I met Yuva when I was seven, and she was to remain my friend till I was twenty. We went to the same school until the time we had to go to different colleges. There were three of us then, but our third friend moved away after a year of us knowing each other, and after that it was just Yuva and me. Pretty and green-eyed, she had light skin and golden brown hair, cut short to the nape of her neck which curled at the ends. For the first few years of school she only wore her cardigan and never the half-sleeved pullover the rest of us wore. Her socks only reached up to her ankles revealing reed like legs that were scaly from not being moisturized. It would be a while before she wore socks that reached up to her knees like how the other girls wore. She carried gooseberries in her skirt pocket and chewed on them throughout the day, popping each one into her mouth when no one was looking. She handed me a fistful every morning before school assembly. We had them in class and immediately drank water afterwards, our tongues sweetened by the aftertaste.

Yuva was my best friend and was nice to everyone else in our class too, but I had to admit that she had always had a problem with stealing and with telling the truth. Some of the other girls in the class suspected sometimes that she was taking things from others, but they never had any proof. Those bullies would throw insults like 'thief' frequently, but without any evidence the other girls did not really know what to make of these accusations.

The first year we were friends Yuva stole from me quite often. The others would accuse her: 'She stole a piece of your banana cake, D, you go check.' Not knowing what was true I often gave her the benefit of the doubt. But I think even if it had been proven that she had stolen from me, I would not have minded. I needed a friend more than I cared about the cake those days.

One time, when we were in the first standard, Yuva took a packet of Cadbury's Gems from my bag and convinced me that our classmate Rachel had done it.

'Let's check everyone's bags while they're out during the lunch break!' she said to me conspiratorially when she saw me dismayed over the loss of my sweet treats. 'I'm sure we will find it,' she said to a very sceptical me.

I had just about convinced myself that I must have dropped the sweets somewhere. 'I don't know...' I replied, feeling uncomfortable.

'You want to know where it went, right? This is how we do that,' she said with an air of surety.

At lunch we went to the empty classroom. Everyone was out in the grounds playing by the swings or slides. There were thirty chairs and tables for the thirty students. The chairs were red and the tables green. The room smelled like a potpourri of wet dog and stale air. We rifled through bag after bag but I did not find my Gems. We went down the rows systematically, and when we finally got to Rachel's bag I found nothing. Just books and her pencil box. In a side pocket of her school bag I found a small clear plastic case in the shape of a heart. It was purple and inside it was a lavender-scented eraser, also in the shape of a heart. I looked at it longingly, remembering how I had seen it in Mr Baruah's store and was too scared to ask my mother to buy one for me. Rachel was snooty and had never let me even look at her eraser when I asked her.

'Take it,' Yuva said as she saw me looking at it longingly and turning it between my fingers. 'She probably stole your Gems anyway. I saw her eat some. They must have been yours.'

I knew it was wrong to take what was not mine. This was stealing, and the better part of my conscience was reeling against the act I was going to commit. My brain felt like it was beginning to bubble like soup in a stockpot, as I thought hard about this. I convinced myself that Yuva knew something I did not.

'You know what, I think you might be right. I think I will take this as revenge, you know,' I heard a distant voice say and it took me a second to realize it was my own. I quickly put the small, heart-shaped eraser into my skirt pocket and we ran out of the room before anyone else saw us.

That evening, the eraser felt heavy in my pocket. I was so busy thinking of where and how to hide that stolen piece of property that I never used it. On reaching home, I kept it in my bag but that was not good enough. I hid it in the drawer of my study table, but I was afraid my mother might see it. So then I went and placed it high up on a shelf in one of my grandmother's guest bedrooms, safely out of sight.

When I noticed that the shelf I had placed it on was where my grandmother kept her spare Bible, I saw this as a sign from God.

The next day, I waited for the girls to go out to play during lunch. When they were out I quietly put the eraser back into Rachel's bag, and that night I slept fitfully. Rachel apparently never noticed.

Yuva stopped stealing from me the second year of our friendship, and then she started lying. She lied about everything. She lied about what she ate for dinner the night before and about how many toys she had. She lied about the clothes she bought and about how many books she had. It came very easily to her. Her eyes never avoided mine when she was lying, nor did she sweat and stutter. She did it confidently; her mother, the teachers and friends never doubting the veracity of her stories. She told us she had every kind of Barbie doll imaginable. Barbies with cars, castles and horses, Barbies that did not even exist. I felt bad about not having as many as she did and would often ask if I could play with hers; she always refused but I never suspected she was lying to me.

Yuva got found out one day when her elder sister Ananta came to play with us during our school lunch break.

'You're so lucky you have all those different fancy Barbies,' I said to Ananta as we sat and played by the swings.

'What different Barbies? We have only one which we share,' she replied, sounding surprised.

I turned to look at Yuva who by then had the most sheepish expression on her face.

'But Yuva said...'

'Eh! She is lying to you,' she said, cutting me off.

Again I looked at Yuva. 'Ha ha! I was just pranking you! Who told you to believe me!' she said.

Her eyes gleamed and she did a twirl when she got caught, like she always did. Like it was always her plan. She never displayed any guilt. I did not know why she had been lying, but we did not speak any more about it. I stopped taking everything Yuva said seriously from that day. As we got older, I could sift through the lies and the truth, and she stopped telling tales to me as often.

Apart from this hamartia, Yuva was kind and empathetic, calling me on the phone whenever she knew I was upset. Her father was a government servant, so she could rake up a high phone bill without getting into trouble. I always waited till my parents were out of the house before I rang her up and asked her to call me back. On the other side of the phone her calm, confident voice was able to help me with my anxieties. For this I was able to ignore her lying habits. 'Don't worry,' would be her soothing refrain when I was sad or had not slept. While everyone around me came to me to tell me their problems, I went to her. She helped me in school when I got into trouble, or when I was trying to avoid the one senior in my school who had a habit of grabbing, groping and tickling me for no reason. Yuva was my lookout whenever she was around. I called her Kafley Girl endearingly when we got older. Kafley was her surname. Her family used to call her Chili. We were inseparable and my earliest memories of school cannot be recollected without her.

Yuva was a pacifist. She never got into fights and hated confrontation, preferring to keep quiet rather than argue. I loved to argue with people and I would urge her to fight alongside me.

'We should fight when people are bullying us. Fight when people are trying to get in the way of our friendship. Fight when people say mean things,' I would insist.

I think I was able to bend her a little because one day she came to me triumphantly and told me what had happened to her on her way to my home. 'You know what happened today?!' She said excitedly.

'What?'

'I showed some boys that they cannot bully me. I was walking home and these cheapster boys said, "Khmat kum ka miaow" to me,' she finished, her face flushed. They were referring to her green eyes, comparing them to a cat's.

'Ani! So annoying!' I exclaimed 'What did you say then?'

'Khmat kum u ksew!' she replied.

'You said that?! You said their eyes were like a dog's?'

'Yes! Because they are brown na! Like a dog's! They were so shocked I understood Khasi and that I could insult them back in Khasi!'

We both started laughing at this. This was a proud moment for her and I patted her on the back just like her father would.

I was easily bored as a child and always came up with games and was getting into mischief. At home I would reel in my cousins, and at school it was Yuva. We came up with code names for genitalia so we could make jokes in the open and giggle. 'Pupa' was one of the terms we used because I thought breasts look like chrysalises. We had been studying the lifecycle of the butterfly then. Once I had convinced a group of my classmates that someone had been murdered in the school football field and that it was a graveyard during the time of the British. All of us took to searching for bones that winter afternoon during the school break. During the summer we hardly got a chance to play outside, so we took advantage of the dry weather. I was convinced there was a body under the large weeping willow that stood by the Principal's cabin. We dug into the mud with sticks, soiling our knees and shirts. We never found anything.

When it rained we sat in the assembly hall and watched the other kids run around playing tag. I ate my soggy sandwiches and she her dry roti; what we could not eat we fed the dogs that walked around inside the school grounds. In that musty hall we talked about wanting to open up an orphanage for dogs, and I convinced her that we could. In the colder months a group of us, including Yuva, walked together in our oversized blazers to the field, sat on the grass and looked up at the sky. We tried to avoid sleeping on pine cones that prodded our backs. Each year, close to winter break, we would plead with our parents to allow us to carry our cameras to school so we could take pictures for memory's sake. Yuva once brought her mini camera and we recorded hundreds of videos.

In our school it was the class teacher who decided who would sit where. This was to ensure that friends never sat together so the class would remain disciplined. Once every two weeks, the teacher called out from the attendance sheet and carefully rearranged the girls as she would flowers in a prized vase. One time the teacher inadvertently placed Yuva and I next to each other, much to our delight. The whole week after consisted of the rest of the class trying to separate us, even snitching on us: 'Miss, they will talk and not pay attention because they're friends,' Joy, the class monitor said.

When the teacher ignored her, the class monitor took it upon herself to change our seats.

'Hey you, you girls, you are friends, you can't sit like this. You go sit there,' she told Yuva, who immediately acquiesced.

'You don't have to go sit there, Yuva, don't listen to her. She isn't the class teacher,' I said vehemently, throwing Joy a dirty look. 'And my name is not "you girl".' But by then the other girls had joined in. They took Joy's side and goaded Yuva into shifting.

'I'm the class monitor, and I'm sure Miss Khongwir picked me because she knew I would stop all this.' Joy and the others goaded and hounded us until Yuva threw me a defeated look and went and sat next to Dimple, the girl who ate her peaches without removing the skin.

The other girls continued this way until we were in the tenth grade. All the while, it never eroded our friendship. All the while, the bullies had not won, frustrated as they had made us feel when we were younger. Sometimes even the teachers joined in, intent on separating Yuva and me, and I felt helpless. I never understood the reason completely. Maybe they were being malicious for the sake of it, and they enjoyed bullying us. When I grew older I thought perhaps it was because she was a non-tribal Nepali girl, and I was Khasi. Perhaps they thought it was unimaginable that we could be such good friends. All the other girls played and ate lunch with people of their own ethnicities. The Bengali girls sat among themselves, the North Indians with the North Indians, Khasis with Khasis, Garos with Garos. Yuva and I stood out for not doing the same.

As we advanced in class, we shifted from classroom to classroom. We stopped thinking about the animal orphanage and spoke about college instead. We spoke of our futures and our wedding dresses. We continued to eat gooseberries under the sun, picked wild berries in the field, staining our white shirts when we kept them in our pockets and shared our tiffins at lunch. I relied on Yuva as I did on the tree that stood in the middle of Barik, which faithfully burst into green every spring after appearing skeletal all winter.

I often went to Yuva's house on the weekends, where we exchanged Nancy Drew novels and made snacks on the coiled electric stove. She lived in a government flat. It was functional, neat and clean. She shared her room with her elder sister, Ananta, and she had two twin brothers who shared a room opposite theirs. Her father was a government servant who would often pat me on my shoulder when he would see me. He was a good sort and always welcoming. He was short and stocky, with a greying mustache that was wilted at the ends. Her mother was a pretty woman, a head taller than her husband. All her children looked like variations of her. She seemed shy and was very quiet, only speaking to me when she had to offer me food.

I loved looking around Yuva's room. She did not keep her clothes in a cupboard but in a trunk underneath her bed. I always made her pull it out because I liked to rummage through it. It fit perfectly under the bed, a large, grey heavy trunk lined with newspaper that filled the air with the smell of mothballs every time she opened it. There were two wooden shelves on the wall where she kept knick knacks and her novels, and below that was a wooden table where she placed all her school books, leaning them against the wall. The sunlight filled the room with warm soothing tones. My favourite part of their house was the terrace. On our winter break, we went up there in the afternoons to soak up the sun. She and her sister took out mattresses and placed them on the floor of the terrace and we lay down on them, our backs to the sun. We sucked on lime pickle, the salt coming onto our chins and noses and the sour taste tingling on our tongues while the pigeons the family fed cooed in the background. Her mom made these pickles, placing them in old Bournvita glass jars.

The rest of the time in her house we spent reading books and comics. Her father subscribed to *Reader's Digest* and would buy their hardbound encyclopaedias. We spent hours going through a book called *The Mysteries of the Unexplained* which had stories of Jack the Ripper, the Chupacabra, the Alligator Man, and the deadly song 'Gloomy Sunday'. We read the book page to page, putting it on our laps, turning glossy page over glossy page. We were fascinated, and I made my mother buy me that book so we could do the same when she came over. Her father had a small snake that he had preserved in an old alcohol bottle, and they hung it on their wall on one side of the sitting room where we sat and read. Her brothers liked to bring it down and present it to me as if I had never seen it before: 'D, have you seen this? Bet you haven't,' one of them said, waving it at me, and I rolled my eyes at them.

On some days, fair weather tempted us into leaving the house and going for a walk. She lived in Cleve Colony, a nice quiet green area perfect for strolls. We inhaled the fresh smell of green and pet the dogs on the street, getting fur on our hands. We crossed large opulent houses on both sides of the road, past the fisheries and deserted government research centres. She lived on a hill and from where we stood outside her gate, we could see the hill on the opposite side with the houses jutting out like colourful graves emerging from the soil. We walked further up past more houses and crossed Tripura Castle. She told me the royal family of Tripura actually lived there, or at least their descendants. I didn't believe her until her sister confirmed it.

'There is a prince; he's very good-looking. He is always driving by in a new motorcycle or car every day. One time he almost ran over Ma and me when we were taking a walk. I wish he had fallen off that stupid motorcycle,' said Ananta disdainfully.

From where we stood on the street, we could not see the inside or the grounds. There was a curved stone arch above the gate that bestowed upon it a certain grandeur. A thin paved road ran up the curved path like the seams of stockings on a woman's leg. I wondered if it led to the castle. One day I walked up the road because I wanted a better look at the castle. Yuva did not let me get far.

'They have fifteen big dogs!' Yuva warned me. 'They're trained to kill!' she said, and I ran back down before I could find out for myself.

On the opposite side of the castle, across the road and down a set of stairs, just off the road, there were the remains of a swimming pool. We could see it from the road. I think this land with the old pool also belonged to them, but it looked abandoned and had gone through several stages of decay and neglect. 'Must be strange to be royalty,' I told Yuva whenever we crossed that place. 'To have so much space, but not the time to look after it all?'

'Yep,' she agreed.

The swimming pool was shaped like an amoeba. There was no water in it and the veneer had begun to fade and chip. The paint was peeling off and had adopted a white, ashen colour. The ground around the pool was covered with fallen and discarded pine leaves that had fallen from the trees that lined the surrounding area. These leaves were dry and had turned brown. They crunched underneath our feet as we walked around the pool. There were so many brown pine leaves on the ground around the pool forming patterns that it looked like a lion's umber-coloured mane when viewed from above. When we were younger, we would collect these leaves and prop them on sticks. We made 'houses' for animals and decorated them with flowers that we picked from the side of the road.

At the end of the road, at the top of the hill, there was the Pastoral Centre. It was quiet there. We went there quite often and sat on the cold stone benches that nestled in the grass. All we could hear were the birds as we breathed in the fresh air, the cold air stinging our eyes and noses and making them water.

'I think I want to be an archaeologist, Yuva,' I turned to her and said one time as we sat there. 'You know I love animals, and there are so many stray dogs and cats, who will save them all? But I also want to go exploring,' I continued, my voice starting to sound strained as I thought of all the helpless animals. I was eleven.

She nodded in agreement.

'I need help if I want to do both. Will you help me start it?' I asked her. 'We can open it up together. We could be like Florence Nightingale from the Ready Reckoner story we were reading last year, remember? But for animals. What do you say?'

'I do like this idea. We should do something like this together. We're best friends so it's only obvious we have to,' she said, as she smiled at me.

'I will need to go on archaeological missions to Egypt and Chile and Sindh, and I will miss the animals but you will be there.'

'Can I come with you then?'

'Yes of course. We will have someone take care of the animals while we're gone. Someone we trust, maybe my sister.'

She agreed and we sat quietly for a while till the crickets came out and the mosquitoes started to gnaw at our legs and hands through our jeans.

We never went there anymore after her sister Ananta told us that she had heard a bear was found roaming those grounds and that it was dangerous.

--

Every year on Diwali I went over to Yuva's house. Diwali was a big deal for Yuva and her family. She and her sister spoke about it for a month before the day. On the day, she had all her relatives over, even her great grandmother, who always peered at me through her thick spectacles and smiled in recognition. As soon as we went into the house we were offered sel roti and coconut ladoos. The sweet smell of coconut always tempted me into taking two, putting one in my handkerchief and one in my mouth. The ghee always soaked through the cloth. The house had diyas at every entrance and corner and the unforgiving smell of uncooked mustard oil made our noses tingle. In Yuva's room we sat on the bed as we talked over each other and balanced the round steel plates in our laps and hands. We dipped the sel roti into a green curry that was not appetizing to look at but was one of the most delicious things I have ever eaten. It was a potato and cucumber gravy that was peppery, and I heaped my plate full of it. The mix of sweet and savoury, much to my initial apprehensions, worked well together. Yuva's mom cooked all of this herself.

Soon I began to take my sister along on my parents' insistence. After dinner, we went to the terrace and burst crackers with her brothers. A metallic smell greeted us outside, and we coughed as our lungs adjusted to the air. The night was hazy from the smoke that came from the burst firecrackers. I pulled my jacket tighter and walked toward the bundle of crackers that lay on the ground. I was particularly scared of the string of small red crackers that burst in quick succession, so I avoided those completely. I settled for the sparkling phuljhari sticks. One year they had bought a string with a hundred of the little red crackers tied together. On their father's instructions, Yuva's brothers burst it outside on the streets in order not to scare anyone at home. When Yuva's father left his guests and came up to the terrace, it meant that the fancy crackers would finally be taken out of their boxes. We all got excited when we saw him appear and could not wait for these rockets to be lit. He was like the chief guest, and we were waiting for him to cut a ribbon.

'Baba, can we light one of these, please?' one of his sons requested as he took the fancy ones out of the plastic bags.

'OK but you better be careful,' he replied as he smiled, watching his son carefully place the candle under the thread to light it. It first sparked and spluttered, catching fire, and then pierced through the grey, hazy air, sweeping through the clouds until it burst and exploded into seven colours, lighting up the sky for a brief moment. In that moment, everyone was excited and quiet, our faces turned to the night sky and the flashing light reflected in our eyes. The Khasi boys prowling the streets would often come and ask Yuva's brothers for crackers to play with, and they happily complied. They wanted to be liked by the local boys. These boys did not think much about Diwali and Ram's grand homecoming, but they loved playing with the crackers, especially the 'chocolate bombs' wrapped in foil. Those were small in size but were always the loudest ones. They liked to put them in tin cans immediately after lighting them to maximize their effect. The 'bomb' would explode inside, cracking the tin open, and the sound of metal rang in our ears for the rest of the night.

—

The winter holidays were when Yuva and I consumed all the novels we had put off reading because of our school exams. After we had both read a book, we met so we could discuss it in detail. We started with idyllic novels of Enid Blyton wishing we were also in boarding school and then moved on to Nancy Drew trying to figure out the mystery before we got to the last chapter. By standard eight, we had moved on to the sappy romance novels, Mills and Boon, that we borrowed from the U Like lending library. We paid fifty rupees as a security deposit and ten for borrowing. We sat there for hours thumbing through the large shelf of romance novels. In class ten, we were reading Danielle Steele and Sidney Sheldon and I would hide these from my father because these were 'not literature', as he told me once. My sister saw me read something called *Darling Deceiver* once, a romance novel about a handsome, washed-up country singer and his intern. She thumbed the yellow pages and made fun of the cover, which had a woman and a man embracing each other. Yuva had discovered it at the lending library. My sister sang the words 'darling deceiver' to made-up melodies every time Yuva came over after that.

My whole family knew Yuva well. Mei would worry

every time she came over, fretfully stating, 'Ani! We cooked beef today.'

'So what? We won't feed her that,' I replied.

'Te, what jingtah will we give her?!' Mei asked, agonized at having to feed her guest rice without gravy.

Every year, except for the year that she was sick, Yuva would come to my grandmother's Christmas dinners. On Christmas, our whole family went to church in the evenings and then assembled at my grandmother's. Yuva loved coming to church with us, and the week before Christmas we talked for hours on the phone, discussing what she and I would wear. We ate ja stem and doh khlieh for dinner and pudding for dessert. My grandmother spent all morning preparing the food, complaining throughout but secretly enjoying the work, I always thought. Nonetheless, Mei made sure we never forgot how much time it took her.

'Consider my age kein pha! Would any other granny do this much?' she asked each year.

'No, not at all. You are really strong and healthy, unlike other grandmothers. That is why you have the energy,' I replied. An answer she always expected, reassuring her like my father used to reassure Mrs Guha.

We sat by the fireplace watching Christmas films on the television, and my aunts sneakily gave us a small glass of wine. My family loved having Yuva over. When we got older, her sister and brother joined us too.

When we were sixteen, my parents expressed surprise that Yuva and I had been friends for so long, and they invited her family over for dinner to get to know them better. Her parents came over, and I was excited because this meant Yuva and I could watch television together at night. That day my mother cooked vegetarian food, not letting anyone help. She spent a long time making dahi vada, while my father tried to sneak away the fried vadas from the hot pan. The dinner went well and only solidified our relationship.

—

By the time we were in our early teens, Yuva and I paid attention in class only when we were fond of the teachers. Most of the time we played games in the back of our notebooks. Every inch of the last two pages of our notebooks was covered in scribbles. Crosses and circles filled nearly all the back pages and we preemptively drew vertical lines on blank pages for the Name, Place, Animal, Thing game. Some pages had notes and dedications. We wrote in each other's notebooks:

> Dear Yuva,
> Don't forget that you are my best friend. You will have to attend my wedding and be my maid of honour. We have to call each other every day when we're grown-up and have jobs. You also have to let me attend your wedding and also design your wedding dress.
> Love,
> D
>
> P.S. If you throw this you will get bad luck for eight years.

Yuva was obsessed with white weddings. After having watched so many films and read so many novels, she had a romanticized idea of the white dress and the walk down the aisle. 'I want to have a Hindu wedding and a white wedding,' she told me one time, looking wistful.

'Then you should marry one of these Khasi boys,' I joked. She kept quiet when I said that. For years after, I felt it was no coincidence that many of the boys she was infatuated with were Khasi.

She replied to my messages:

Dear D,
I will surely come for your wedding and you come to mine. I am looking forward to seeing your ideas and designs. I hope you don't forget to invite me. Also don't worry too much in life.
Love
Kafley Girl

P.S. Don't worry.

At the end of the year, when we were done with our sixth year in school and just before we went on our winter holidays, Yuva got very sick. She skipped school for a week which was unusual for her because she was never absent. She hardly ever got coughs and colds, unlike me. On the phone she downplayed her sickness, telling me to take proper notes at school so she could borrow them. Days went by, but she did not return to school. I was worried for her because the end of year school exams were nearing.

At first, Yuva's parents tried to cure her using home remedies to treat a malady they did not understand. Then they took her to the homeopathic doctor. His clinic was in the Iewduh near the bus stand that reeked of urine, and its walls were graffitied by spittle. My mother used to take me there when I had a cold. I loved eating the crunchy sweet crystals that came in the small glass vials.

'Doctor, don't I need that other medicine?' I asked,

referring to the powder that tasted like Glucon D, which came in little paper packets.

'Keep quiet,' my mother hissed.

The homeopathic medicine did me no good, and I thought of them as snacks. It did Yuva no good either, because she did not get better.

Her parents admitted her to a proper hospital when she kept getting worse. They gave her drug after drug, conducted test after test but remained baffled. She just got sicker and had to stay in the hospital for days. I went to visit her soon after she was hospitalized. I sat at the side of her bed in the hospital room. The white of the room was unnerving, the floors smelled sanitized and lemony, the nurse kept coming in to check the drip, flicking it with her finger and giving me disapproving glances. I brought Yuva a couple of packets of juice, a big chocolate bar, and Betty and Veronica comics for her to read. She smiled weakly when she saw me, and we sat and spoke about what was happening in school.

'Oh you know what? Miss Purkayastha likes to read dirty romance novels! I found her reading a Jackie Collins novel!' I told her.

'Oh what? Those books are filthy!' she exclaimed.

'I know, right?! The other teachers take those books away from us, and here she is reading one in front of us.'

'Was she reading it out in the open?'

'No she covered it up with a newspaper,' I said and we sniggered.

I could not go to visit Yuva as often as I wanted to, but I went whenever I got a chance. Her health continued to deteriorate, and she seemed to wither. Her skin had dark patches that no one could explain, and she told me that when she tapped on these patches of skin they made a hollow sound. 'Like tapping wood,' she showed me. She was afraid the splotches made her look bad.

People in school started to ask questions about Yuva's absence. During the school assembly the headmistress announced, 'One of our own is very sick. She needs our prayers, girls.' That day, the prayer that accompanied the Lord's Prayer was longer than usual.

In class one morning, when we were reading out of the suggestion box, someone stood up and suggested the class present Yuva a book to make her feel better. 'We can all collect money Miss, and then we can get a card where we can all write messages.'

'Such a good idea,' the class teacher gushed.

I felt stupid that I had not come up with the suggestion. I was her best friend and should have been the one who came up with the idea, I thought to myself. It was suggested that the class monitor collect the money and the teacher purchase the book. They gave me the task of handing over the gift. Each girl in the class wrote 'Get well soon' in the card followed by their name, everyone's handwriting legible enough for Yuva to know who had signed. I went to give her this book, feeling important at having been tasked with this. I carried an extra book for her, one I had bought with my pocket money. She felt gratified that her name was mentioned in the assembly and that the class had bought her a book, and I was happy for it. It must have been terrible to sit on the bed hooked to the drip machine, I thought.

When they saw that the doctors at this hospital were unable to help her, Yuva's parents grew worried and they took her to Vellore. They hoped the doctors there, with their many years of experience in those big, shiny, intimidating buildings, would find a solution. The family took a three-day train ride to Vellore where Yuva sat on another hospital bed with its white sheets and sanitized floors. She was gone most of the winter holiday. She even missed my birthday. I was turning twelve that year and, after hounding my mother into letting me, I threw a birthday party. Yuva could not come, which made both of us sad. On my birthday she called me from the hospital phone. 'Happy Birthday D! I'm sorry I can't be there,' she told me. I could hear her crying on the other side.

'Ni Kafley! I will have one next year. Don't worry. You concentrate on getting better,' I reassured her.

'I thought I'd be better by now,' she said.

'I thought so too.'

We were both quiet for a while. We had planned my party together, hoping she would be back home by then. I listened to her as she continued. She wished she was back home, her voice weak, despairing that she could not do the things she wanted to.

'I'll miss celebrating my birthday with you as well,' she lamented. We were the same age, with just nineteen days separating our birthdays. I tried my best to make her feel better, but I already missed her terribly.

The doctors in Vellore soon found out what she had. She called to tell me, almost relieved to be able to name the insidious monster that was eating away at her health. 'Non Hodgkin's Lymphoma,' she told me, spelling it out steadily, pronouncing each syllable with care. I did not know what that was. 'It's a type of cancer,' she continued.

'It sounds bad,' I said to Yuva. I heard the word 'cancer' and was worried, but only briefly. Only old people died of cancer, not young girls who were barely thirteen, I thought.

I was certain she would be fine, that we would soon be sitting on her terrace eating pickled limes again.

'Oh at least it isn't Hodgkin's Lymphoma,' she joked.

'Come soon,' I told her. 'I have so many books to give you!'

'Yes, I will. I'm sick of being sick.'

While Yuva was away I continued the same routine. I went to school, tuitions and then back home. I struggled with my arithmetic and Hindi. On the weekends I went to my grandmother's or stayed at home. She, in the meanwhile, got blood test after blood test, chemo session after chemo session.

I grew restless without Yuva around. We could not talk on the phone, and I made a mental note of all the amusing things that happened in school so I could tell her about them when she was back. She missed the start of school, and the teachers had pressed ahead with lessons even though she was missing. But finally, at the end of five long months, she called to tell me she was cured.

'I can't wait to be back home. Gosh! it has been so long,' she said, her voice sounding relieved.

'Oh man! How many days will it take for you to get back?' I asked impatiently.

'It takes three days by train.'

'See! Told you you would get better,' I said. The doctors in the shiny intimidating buildings had proved themselves to be worth the praise.

The day she arrived back in Shillong, we were both very excited and spoke on the phone for hours as we planned what we would do when we met, hanging up the phone only after my mother started yelling at me to go to sleep. The next day I woke up early and quickly got ready to leave. I finished my chores, got dressed hurriedly, and my father drove me to Yuva's house. I crossed the haunted house she swore she saw a ghost in one time and the small stall she bought milk from. Outside her house, her father and mother sat in the sun eating soh phi and salt from a small bowl. They greeted me warmly. I had not been here in months, but it all looked the same: the dimly-lit corridor, the smell of her mother's mango pickle and incense burning in the little temple by the stairs. Nothing had changed.

I walked toward Yuva's bedroom. Before I could knock, a girl came out of the room and smiled at me. She said, 'Hi.'

I replied, 'Hello, can you tell me where Yuva is?'

She looked at me, grinning. 'D, it's me, Yuva!'

I looked at her, startled. She sounded like Yuva but looked nothing like her. This girl was chubby and bald. Her cheeks were so full that when she smiled they eclipsed her eyes. Her hands and feet looked swollen. There were no upturned curls and thin scrawny legs. No small face and lanky arms. The girl who stood before me was someone who looked so different that it was inconceivable to me that she was my old friend.

'You're not Yuva!' I said in disbelief, but then I hesitated and leaned in close to see her eyes. They were the same, green like the gooseberries she ate.

After a moment, Ananta came out to see me. I looked at her for reassurance. 'Ah, you both are reunited at last,' she said.

'But Yuva! You have changed so much!' I said, astonished.

'Arey, come in at least. Sit down. Let us chit-chat,' she said, smiling at me and patting me hard on the back.

We sat in that same familiar room, on that same familiar bed. I breathed in the smell of nail varnish and detergent.

I swung my feet, and they hit the tin trunk underneath. I looked around and saw the books we had given her, next to some new ones. The pages at the edges were all curled up. Ananta came in with Tang and some chips, and we sat and spoke after what felt like ages.

'It's the medicine. It made me gain weight. It also made me lose my hair. It will grow back,' she told me, almost reassuring me as if I was the one who was sick and suffering.

'Yes yes, of course. I was just shocked, that's all,' I said, happy to be sitting there. I squeezed her hand, and she laughed that same familiar laugh.

'I knew you'd react like that.'

While we sat and sipped Tang, she told me about the treatments she had undergone. Test after test, injection after injection until they finally found out what was wrong. 'The biopsy was the worst,' she said. She described scissors cutting chunks of skin and a tube being inserted into her arm, and I cringed at the thought and shivered in that warm sunlit room.

'Were you scared?' I asked her, knowing that I could not even go to the dentist without feeling anxious.

'I grew tired of being prodded and poked like an animal in a laboratory. But at least I am not scared of injections anymore,' she joked.

I managed a weak smile.

'The thing is, the doctors at the hospital in Shillong did not know what they were doing. They gave me medicines for typhoid and jaundice and all sorts of things. Those medicines made me worse, and the doctors in Vellore had to pump all these out,' Yuva continued. I felt angry on hearing this. 'I'm so sick of medicine and needles,' she said.

'Ni lah palat these doctors! They poisoned you! I'm glad

they finally found out what was wrong, though,' I said. I felt terrible for her. She was so changed and had gone through so much, but she spoke in a way that ensured she did not seem pitiable.

When she came back to school everyone wanted to speak to her. She was like a celebrity, and I felt like her bodyguard. I told people to back off when they got too close or asked too many questions. I felt possessive of her.

Outside school we continued as usual, sharing books and talking about our futures. We walked up to the swimming pool, and she told me how on one occasion her mother had called someone to explain if there was some other reason why their daughter was sick. Something supernatural is what many in her family believed was the cause of her sickness.

'A pandit told my Mom that I was getting ill because of spirits,' she said, as we walked and ate the Wai-Wai her father had brought for her from Nepal.

'What does that mean?'

'You see that hill over there,' she said as she pointed to a hill far off, opposite the front of her house.

'Yes, that one, right?' I pointed and nodded as I looked at a hill that was probably part of Malki.

'Well, apparently, there was a boy who lived there who fell in love with a girl who lived on that hill. She died before they could get married. The boy died soon after she did. He died of a broken heart.'

'What's that got to do with you?'

'Apparently the spirit of the boy comes out in the evenings to look for the girl on this hill. He would try to spot her from the hill he was on, every evening at dusk. They say I look like her, and I always take evening walks. He must have mistaken me for her.'

'Are you saying people think a ghost made you sick?' I asked.

'Yeah, something like that. That the spirit caused it by looking at me. I don't quite get how it works. Anyway, whatever caused it, I'm better now,' she said, smiling.

We sat on the side of the pool until it got dark, dangling our legs as we finished the rest of the Wai-Wai.

Our last few years in school became about matching our temperaments to the right people. This took a toll on all of us as we contended with our maturing bodies, our attitude towards the opposite sex and our growing irritation with our elders. This confusion was further compounded by competition we felt with the other girls in class. 'Oh that girl is so much prettier than me'; 'She has had three boyfriends, and I have had only one'; 'How can she juggle studies and a boyfriend?' These were the words that came out of all our mouths. Matters that we would have considered frivolous seemed so important. When we were younger, we did not have to contend with worries about our looks, boys or how we were perceived by others in the school. We never worried about who was smarter, who came from money, or social standing, like we did now.

By the time we got to the ninth standard our group had swelled in number. From two in first standard, we became four in seventh standard, to six in ninth standard and then finally eight. First it was just Yuva and me. Lucy joined us in third standard, then Annie came along in seventh standard, followed by Sara. Our little group grew again when Priya and Shreeja joined us in eight standard. Varsha came last, when her father was transferred to Shillong. Although we were all of differing temperaments, Yuva was the glue that held us together. Then the worries that came with our maturing senses of selves in the wake of puberty seemed to push through the cracks. Things became complicated; we had to deal with confusing feelings and ideals that were shaped along the way. The girls in our group of friends stopped seeing things the same way. We eventually did split up because one half of the group, mostly the non-tribal girls, thought they were 'too different' and wanted to go their own way.

'You're fine, Yuva, you could have come and been in our group,' I heard them comfort her as she cried, devastated by their decision to go their separate way.

'Those girls are just not like us. We like to discuss intellectual things you know,' the snootiest of those girls told her. I always felt that they did not want to be friends with us anymore because the rest of us were tribal.

'We would have called you over to our group, but we know we cannot break you and D apart.' Priya said.

Yuva tried to convince them to change their mind but they would not. I called her away. 'Leave these girls, Yuva. They're just plain mean,' I said, feeling terrible on seeing the anguished look on her face. She was upset over this for months while I was unperturbed by their strange elitism. We were there for each other then.

Our last two years in the higher secondary school saw us getting mobile phones, and we were allowed to venture out to house parties. Yuva and I were able to convince our parents to let us get contact lenses. We both felt ugly and unattractive in our spectacles. We began to put kajal under our eyes and took trips to Glory's Plaza, the Tibetan clothes market, on our own without adult supervision. We browsed through stacks of badly stitched clothes and when we were done we ate hot momos in the stall on the top floor. We squeezed in on the painted red chairs and ate red chutney that burnt our lips and caused our noses to run.

The cherry blossoms came like they did every year, but they did not look as brilliantly pink as they had when we were younger. By this time, Yuva and I had begun to drift apart. I had begun to phase her out of my life. For me, she symbolized my childhood and hence formed part of my childhood identity, an identity I wished to refashion as I grew older. I wanted to be perceived as another type of adult, one who had shed away parts of my past that I found wanting. That me was an old me, a me I did not particularly like as an eighteen-year-old. I wanted to be the kind of girl who did well in school and still managed to look pretty enough to get a boyfriend, regardless of whether I really wanted one. I saw Yuva as a hindrance to me forging this new persona. I would say mean things about her behind her back to the other girls. I did not understand why I did this at first. I started to get irritated that she was always around, and when she was not, I felt lonely. When we were in twelfth standard, I felt she was not as 'hip' as some of the other girls and that being associated with her would make me 'uncool'. I laughed at her, talking about her having body odour as if it were the worst thing in the world.

I was not proud of what I said. I felt overcome with shame after I said those terrible things, and I would find a nicer way to say these things to her to stifle any guilt. But still, I started to replace her with other girls in my class, tiring of her like one would an old toy. Another rift came between us when she was chosen to be a prefect at the beginning of the school year when we turned seventeen. Although I was happy for her, I felt left out when she would go do important things and attend meetings. She told me only much later that she used to feel the same when she was never chosen for the choir, and I would go for practice.

--

The year we passed out of school, the cherry blossoms that bloomed looked almost white. They were as lacklustre as my friendship with Yuva then.

She had decided to study in a college different from mine, and I was pleased that we would finally be apart. I hoped that the space would help us renew the bond that had perhaps been ruptured by proximity. The distance did bring us together again, and we became closer than before. I came to understand I could not separate her from my adult self just as I could not separate her from my childhood self. I accepted her as my totem.

Yuva studied Economics on my suggestion. Although we were studying in separate colleges, my college was close to hers, and I would walk through it when I was done with class, on my way back home. At her college, we sat in the shade under the trees, next to a coffee stand. Coffee spilled from the foam cups that we sometimes accidentally crushed in our hands. Palomino restaurant was nearby on the roadside, where we ordered the cheapest thing on the menu, parathas. Couples and cute boys in chequered shirts came in and went out. Young, poor children carrying jholas filled with posters of Jesus and quotes from the Bible came to our tables, begging and persuading us to buy something: 'Thied seh Kong'. We watched them all, sitting there till it got dark. She told me of the boy in her class she liked. His name was Rob, and he had long hair. I teased her about it.

He played the guitar, was part of a band and sang in church. She liked him for a while, and we would sit near the gate pretending we were minding our own business as we waited for him to come there to get his scooter. As he walked by we waved at him, elbowing each other's ribs. It did not work out between them, and she was sad about it for a long time.

Towards the end of the first year of college I felt I had been finally inducted into true adulthood. I started dating someone. The worry I had about being unattractive dissipated for a bit. I began to have other worries like my peers. 'Oh when do we begin holding hands?' 'How often can I text without looking desperate?' Questions like these occupied a large chunk of my mind. Yuva was there to help me talk myself out of my baseless anxieties. We both thought we would find boyfriends at the same time, and I was sad she did not have one as well. A part of me felt like I had left her behind, but she was glad at my fortune. 'I'm so happy for you,' she told me. 'But now you won't have time for me anymore,' she said jokingly, a tinge of sadness in her eyes.

'Don't be silly. I will always have time for you,' I reassured her.

My having a boyfriend never changed anything. Yuva still came over all the time. We exchanged books, talked about boys, and my grandmother still fretted about how she had made beef and that there was no jingtah for Yuva.

In time, Yuva began to complain that she was not doing very well with her course. 'Economics is too difficult, and I cannot understand what the teacher is saying,' she complained to me. 'I need to change my subject.'

She told me she was applying to different colleges, outside Shillong, and that her father had agreed to her decision. I did not believe her, I refused to. 'We will talk about it when you get in,' I said, being evasive when she wanted to discuss it. I felt it was like one of those lies she told when we were younger and that there was no way she would leave Shillong.

One evening as we sat on the stairs by the coffee shop, watching students filing out of their rooms as the rain beat down hard against the roof of that sheltered nook, Yuva told me she had got into another college in Mumbai. She would be leaving soon. My stomach lurched and I ignored her.

'Did you hear me, D? I'm serious.'

I turned to look at her. 'Are you really telling the truth?', I asked suspiciously.

'Yes. This is my last month here. I'm going to study law in Mumbai.'

'Why? Stay here no; why do you want to leave?' I whined.

'I don't, but I can't keep up with the classes here,' she said, sounding apologetic.

'Okay next month na, let's see next month,' I said and pushed it out of my mind.

It had been a month since we had joined the second year. In August, the monsoons were unrelenting. It rained and thundered in the mornings, and the sky cleared by the evening time, only for the rain to start again at night. By the time class was over, we could walk without our umbrellas to the aloo muri stand and wait for the guy to whip up our orders. The sunset over these clouds rendered them an orange hue that looked brilliant against the sky. If the rain never stopped in the evenings, we usually went back home or had tea at my grandmothers.

At this time we were only settling in at college. Yuva had started getting ready to leave. She began to pack her things and complete administrative formalities at her old college. I saw then that this was very real. She was actually leaving. I was able to put aside my feelings and went shopping with her, helping her prepare for her move to the big city.

On the last day before she left, Yuva invited a few of her close friends over. We drank tea and ate Maggi with chilli flakes in it. Everyone talked and laughed, giving her advice and wishing her luck. I could not hear them, I kept looking at my watch every few minutes, wishing I could stop time by staring at it hard enough. I refused to believe she was going to go. When it began to grow dark someone got up to indicate that it was getting late. Yuva walked down with us all the way to the kirana store which stood next to Mizoram House. There we said our goodbyes.

'Don't forget me, okay?' she said to Luna, a new friend she had made during her short time in college. 'You better call me every day,' she sniffled.

'Ni this one! Kong of course I will,' she said as she hugged her tightly.

'All of you keep in touch with me,' Yuva threatened as she hugged each one there. That evening the clouds were the same popsicle orange they were every evening; the road was wet from the rains, and the tree that leaned against the kirana store dripped rainwater onto our heads. As she hugged our friends one by one I saw Yuva's hair glisten in the sun. It had grown so long and had become a brown three shades lighter after it grew back since her illness. She had changed, so had I.

When she was done hugging everyone she looked at me. We felt cold as we both pulled at our sweaters, and we shuddered as we tried to avoid getting hit by a stray ball from the boys who were playing cricket on the street. I delayed the goodbye as long as I could. I felt awkward as the others watched us finally hug. We screamed together at the same time. No words, just an 'Arghhhh.' The same sound, the same tune, the same pitch, stopping at just the same time. That is all we said. There was nothing we could say that would convey our thoughts and feelings most effectively. After almost thirteen years of being with each other, this.

When she got to Mumbai, Yuva called me and told me that she missed home. 'I don't see the hills when I look out of the window, I only see building after building. It's just so concrete. I don't like it,' she said, sounding sad.

I would comfort her as best as I could. We spoke on the phone frequently those days, planning together how we would spend her Diwali holidays when she was back. This helped her a bit as she felt isolated being away from her family and friends.

But our plans did not work out. Yuva never came back to Shillong for Diwali that year. She got sick.

She called me and told me, and we were both upset. 'I got sick again ya D,' she said, her voice low.

'What?! Sick? How?' I shouted into the phone, my heart racing.

'I am not sure but they are taking me to Tata Memorial.'

'Oh, okay. Will you get better by the time Christmas comes?'

'Yeah, I think so. Don't worry.'

Yuva was sick again for a long while. It was a relapse of the cancer. She had to stay in Mumbai for treatment. She told me again how she was 'sick of being sick', and I felt terrible. It was just an inconvenience, I tried to reassure her. 'Don't worry, you'll be back here soon. Focus on getting better.'

Yuva's cancer consumed her life, like it had earlier. Before she was hospitalized, she was to act in a play that her college was staging at a fest. She had been very excited about it, and she had to put that off now because of her illness. She never complained. I never asked her if she was scared. We never spoke about death. She only told me how she was sick of injections and never said anything about being afraid. At twenty, like at twelve, we did not think about our own mortality. I went to church where we spoke of an afterlife, but for me it was a worry that would come only with old age and grey hair. We believed Yuva would get better.

On our friend Lucy's birthday, Yuva called to wish her. It was October. She had left in May. Yuva's sister called me and told me that speaking to Lucy had upset Yuva and that I was to call her immediately. I called Yuva and asked her what had happened.

'No, it was nothing,' she said, her voice sounding hoarse, but she was laughing.

'Arey, tell me,' I insisted.

'Lucy was going on and on about how I don't deserve to be sick. That I'm a good person, and I should not be going through this. She then started crying, so I started crying. We were both bawling over the phone.' Yuva sighed on the phone. 'I had just called to wish her a happy birthday.'

'What? Oh god, this Lucy is so emotional. She should not have upset you like this.'

'I don't think she meant to.'

'I'm giving her a piece of my mind right now,' I said angrily.

'Leave it D, it's fine.'

'You're being really calm through all this. You're sick and you're handling this better than any person I know. People get sick, don't worry too much. You will be fine, I know it,' I told her. 'Listen, I've already told the jhaal muri guy that when you're back we want the good stuff, and we will be coming to him everyday. No filling the chaat with just muri—big pieces of potato only, I told him.'

'Oh man, yeah, I'd really like that,' she said, beginning to laugh. I could feel her smile over the phone.

'You're the best, and you'll get better. I know it. You got better the last time. Don't listen to that crazy Lucy,' I said, trying to assure myself as I assured her.

We spoke almost every day. Some days she felt better, and on some days she was too sick to talk on the phone. I attended some classes and bunked others, preferring to sit outside on the basketball court of my college as my friends smoked. While I lounged in the sun with my friends, Yuva was getting several sessions of chemotherapy far away in Mumbai. The treatment made her feel weak, but she never told me these things. She never told me about the vomiting and the hair loss. She never told me about how she felt weak and tired. How she felt lonely on the hospital bed, her back aching from lying down too long. She must have been scared, but she never told me. I would only find out she had felt this way later.

For my part, I did not want to ask because asking her if she was scared made her illness more tangible. Then we would have to address it, and I preferred talking to her instead about how she would come back for holidays and the fun we would have together. It was much better to gossip over the phone about our friends than to talk about what medicines she had had that day or the tests she had undergone. I never knew if she preferred that too. She did not tell me. In my mind, she was going to get better, and this would be a little blip in our lives that we would soon set aside. She was not going anywhere, she had my wedding to attend.

Unlike Yuva, my boyfriend at the time, Daniel, could come home for Christmas. His arrival was able to quell some of my disappointment at Yuva's absence. The evening after he arrived, we met outside my grandmother's house when he picked me up. We went for lunch to Laitumkhrah to a restaurant that was frequented by college students. In the winter this place was usually empty, owing to the fact that most of the students who were from the other North Eastern states like Nagaland or Mizoram had gone back home for the holidays, Shillong being an educational hub. At the restaurant we squeezed into the small booth and scarfed down chicken noodle soup and momos. Our mouths were already letting out steam because it was so cold outside. Once we had eaten we went back to his house to watch a film, and our friend Gary joined us. We walked to his house, moving our arms vigorously as we did to generate heat. It got dark early in the evenings in the winter and I was glad for it because I worried my mother might see me. The dark provided good enough camouflage, and we made sure we took the more scenic side routes, where withered trees lined the roads next to pretty houses.

I left my mobile phone at home that day. At five in the evening, as we walked back to my grandmother's, the only light was coming from the stars and people's houses. We climbed up the slope, our breath fogging up in the cold like smoke from a chimney. On the way there I grazed my arm against the grill of a home's exterior fencing and decided that I would get home and clean the wound.

On reaching my grandmother's home, I went in to look at my phone. I had thirty-five missed calls and twenty messages. I panicked and frantically scrolled through the messages.

'Yuva has just passed away,' one of the messages read.

Small, digital text in black against a white background. It shone through the bright screen. This was a flip phone, which my mother bought for me after much haggling. It was orange and weighty and soon after that I began to consider that phone my 'unlucky' phone.

I learnt about my best friend's death through this short message that I received from one of her brothers. The casualness of a text message belittling the news. That is not how one is to learn these things. I looked for answers in the remaining nineteen messages. In a haze, I glanced through them cursorily. Some were from my panic-stricken mother who was angry I had not taken my phone with me. Some were from my sister telling me, 'Mom is freaking out! Where are you?' I was not allowed to go out with boys, and my sister was my lookout.

The rest read 'Where are you?', 'Pick up your phone', 'This is urgent! Call me!'

My head was spinning and on taking a minute to process this, I slowly grasped what I had read. I broke down, and my youngest cousin, who was then eight, ran to my grandmother to tell her.

'Balei?! Lah jah aiu?' Mei questioned my cousin, asking her what had happened. My cousin whispered the news into her ears. I cried hot tears as my grandmother walked around the house, moaning, 'Ani ko blei! She is too young!' She called my mother and my aunts.

In the meanwhile, I gathered strength and returned the calls I had received. I called other friends who were shocked by this news. I was greeted by a series of 'But she was fine a week ago'. I received call after call. Message after message. It never stopped.

I had spoken to Yuva barely a week ago. I remembered telling her she would get through it and beat the cancer. 'Kafley girl, don't worry about it. You are strong; you will be fine in no time,' I had reassured her.

'I hope so,' she replied, her voice sounding weak and very far away.

I was in my backyard when we last spoke. I was soaking up sunshine, my back to the sun as I pulled out weeds from where the coleus grew. She was in a hospital bed, lying on her side, supporting the phone with her pillow. Her back hurt from being on it too long, she had told me. She was bored but not in the way I was. She could not get up from her hospital bed, and she told me she would give anything to do something as menial as pulling out weeds. It was not cold where she was, it was hot. The only thing she liked about it was that the women sometimes wore flowers in their hair. She missed the cold. That is what we had spoken about.

The night after Yuva passed, I went to her house. I went up the same familiar road accompanied by a heaviness that was unfamiliar to me. From the gate I could see people everywhere, sitting at the top and bottom of the stairs. At the entrance sat her old grandmother who smiled at me through her thick frames and said, 'Chili ki friend' and nodded as she put her soft, gnarled hands to my cheek. I smiled at her.

Inside I met her father and mother who were putting on a brave face. Her father patted me on the back when he saw me, like always. Softer this time, like he had weakened. He smiled and went back into the room, nodding as he went along. I was told later that seeing me made him feel sadder. I reminded him of her.

The house was the same, yet not the same. The same smell, the small dimly-lit corridor, the same bright bedroom. This was the first funeral I had been to that was not that of a relative. In the home where a Khasi funeral was held, our noses were always accosted by the smell of smoke from burning wood. Cooks sat outside the house in the backyard over steaming vats of ja stem and doh cooking for the guests who had come to pay their respects. The young kids of the family were all tasked with carrying large aluminium kettles full of tea; there was an option of sha saw or sha dud, depending on what kind of tea they preferred. Younger kids who could not carry the kettles carried trays of butter biscuits making sure no one stayed hungry as they gossiped and lamented. It was like a circus for us then, almost enjoyable because we met friends and cousins, and the adults were too busy to be bothered about us. 'If the food is good in funerals, that's a bad thing,' a friend had told me once about a superstition she knew.

The atmosphere here in Yuva's house was different. There was no hustle and bustle of teapot-bearing children, no smell of doh jem wafting through the air or cooks asking for more wood. Upstairs in the terrace sat all my school friends, talking in solemn whispers. There was no mattress on the floor, no lime pickle. They nodded at me, and I went and sat with them. The air was heavy with grief, and no one spoke. The winter sun burnt our backs, and we drank sweet tea from small cups. I was exhausted from feeling so many different emotions. I felt like a dam that was full and needed its waters to be let out slowly. Ananta was busy with her mother helping guests. One of Yuva's brothers came and kept us company for a while.

'Her heart could not take it. The chemotherapy had weakened her. She could not even pump blood into her own eyelids. They had to tape them shut,' he told me.

I listened, horrified. I imagined her lying down on the bed, alone, her eyes taped shut.

'On the last day she told my dad he had to let her go, but how could he?' he continued, 'She smiled and told him "let me go" over and over. We knew she was in pain. She remembered you too, D.'

'She's not in pain anymore,' a friend of ours remarked softly.

'Yes,' he said, and we all nodded.

A lot of people were there. People from school and college. There was the guy from college who had fallen in love with her, but who she had chosen to remain only friends with. There were our old school teachers, who asked, 'Is D there? Is she alright?'

When it was all over, and the guests had all filtered out, Ananta motioned to me to come to her room. 'I have something Yuva wanted me to give you,' she said. 'I cannot give it to you right now because there are too many people, but come again another day when we have fewer relatives around.' I nodded.

I never went to Yuva's cremation. Days later, I went to their house one last time. I climbed up to their front door and rang the bell. Ananta called me in and ushered me into her bedroom, the one she had shared with Yuva. I sat on the bed and looked around. Many things had been removed and there was a big carton box by the side of the bed. Ananta offered me tea which I accepted.

We spoke little. When we were done sipping our tea, Ananta placed in my hands an old plastic bag as delicately as she would have placed a baby. Inside the bag were notebooks of varying sizes. They were Yuva's diaries. There were so many of them. She had been writing them since we were thirteen. All the years of her life documented in her scrawling handwriting, all she never told me and could never tell. They were all planner diaries that were her father's. Her father, a government servant, never had to worry about there being a shortage of planners.

I touched the suede one at the top, the sides worn out, and opened the pages. I touched the writing and felt the bumps on the paper where the pen had been used too enthusiastically. 'Not here,' Ananta said. I closed the book, sat with her for a while longer, paid my regards to her parents and went back home.

As soon as I got home, I opened the diaries and read them as quickly as I could, afraid the words would turn to dust like she had. While reading I saw a side to her she had been so reticent about. In those tactile pages I read about a Yuva I was unfamiliar with and one I hardly knew. I was learning about a new aspect of her I wish I had known before. Her insecurities accosted me at every page: boys who never liked her back, being bad at singing, having a hard time with college. They all seemed so trivial now.

Her pubescent musings seemed so relatable as I read them. We worried about the same things. Each page chronicling her anxieties. She wanted to be loved and admired. She feared she was unworthy. Her laments about not having a boyfriend were never about their inability to see her worth, but about her inadequacies as a girl. I made small appearances in these chapters, most of them positive. I was glad for proof that she was fond of me because after her death I could only remember bossing her around, worrying that I was a terrible friend.

She wrote very little about her illness, which led me to believe that even she thought she would pull through. Her only mention of it was about being sad she was stuck in a hospital bed. Her friends were out going to house parties and holding hands with boys while she was undergoing chemotherapy.

Each year at school, a book fair was held on the school grounds organized by the St Pauline's bookstore. Yuva and I had loved it. We never had enough money to buy all the books we wanted, but we always had enough for at least one. One year, I picked up a book called *Lisa*. It was an epistolary novel about a girl who had leukaemia. I never finished the novel because I thought it was boring at that time, but I remember lending it to Yuva who read the whole book. I thought of the book often when I thought about Yuva. She had convinced me to buy it, and that was the first time I had read anything about cancer. I should have finished the book before I lost the copy. Then maybe I would have known more about what it felt like to live with cancer. Then maybe, in reading Lisa's account of her battle, I would have better understood what Yuva was going through.

Cancer does not kill twenty-year-old girls, is what I thought then. I know that the eponymous Lisa of the book had survived. Cancer killed adults and old people. I refused to believe Yuva would not get better, just as I had refused to believe she would leave Shillong. She proved me wrong both times.

This was the first time someone I cared about had died. Someone who I had spent almost every waking minute with, all through my childhood and young adult life. I knew I had to grieve, but I did not know where to start. I strung together memories of our times together and wept for a time I could not get back. I also lamented for the future we had hoped for, that would now never be. My grief oscillated between the two.

In later years, my grief began to give way to a numb sadness that sat with me when I happened to see something that triggered her memory. When I got my first job, when I got married, when I first had sex. All these things I would have told her first. I always told her things first.

--

It was a tough Christmas the year that Yuva died. We had both thought she would be there. I fought with my mother a lot after her death. She could not understand how to deal with a daughter who has undergone loss. I also argued a lot with my boyfriend at the time. There was no one to talk to, no one to empathize, and the only one who could was scattered in the wind.

I cannot go back home now and not think of Yuva. To me, she is as much Shillong as the hail that coats the grass every monsoon, the winds that shake loose the tin roofs off people's houses in March and the cherry blossoms that come in November.

The boy on the other hill had seen her, as she walked to the shop to buy milk, her pockets full of gooseberries, a novel tucked under her arm. She did so every evening and tempted fate each time. The sibylline pandit saw this and, dismissing him, we all thought she would get well. She escaped the first time. The second time she did not.

There would be no more leisure walks, jhaal muri and talks of the future with our feet dangling over the old swimming pool. No scribbled notebooks and games of Name, Place, Animal, Thing. She was like the butterflies I had trapped with Bah Rit. Everyone had tried to overturn the jar, her father, her siblings, and even me. We all tried to save her, but it was too late. She was gone, but she left pieces of herself in those diaries, pieces of herself in those pigeons she fed on her terrace, and I am but one of those many pieces she left behind.

Acknowledgements

Thank you to Adhiraj Singh for encouraging me to write this and for helping me make it a better novel.

Thank you to Rigved Siriah who taught me how to edit and shave off excess.

Thank you to my editor Meghna Singh, and the team at Zubaan for believing in this novel.